Amina

Comes to Harlem

A novel by

Sidi

Published by

Harlem Book Center, Inc.
129 West 137th Street, 1B
New York, NY 10030
Tel: +1/646-739-6429

Warning!
This is work of fiction. All the characters, incidents and dialogues are
the products of the author's imagination and are not to be construed
as real. Any references or similarities to actual events, entities, real people, living or dead, or to real locales are intended to give the novel a
sense of reality. Any similarity in other names, characters, entities, places
and incidents is purely coincidental.

Cover Design/Graphics: www.mariondesigns.com
Editor: Barbara Colasuonno

© Copyright 2008
ISBN: 978-0-9800822-0-3

ACKNOWLEDGEMENTS

First of all, I'd like to thank Allah for allowing me to complete this project. To my beautiful family, thanks for being patient with me while my mind was concentrating on getting this novel done.

To my people running the book business in the streets, Omar Traore "Rubbish" from 125th Street, Tony Brown, Balde, Ishmael Sangnan, Massamba Amar Jamaica (Queens), Mustapha, Konate Moriba "le Gouru", Yigo Aboubacar, Abdou Boussou, Abo Ndiaye, 23th Street, 6Ave, Cheikhona Ba, 44th Street, Lex. And a special thanks to the two beautiful models, Sidibe Ibrahime "Papito" and Maimouna Ouedraogo "Mai La Princesse".

Special thanks to: J P Morgan Chase Bank-Harlem, Branch 61, Sean Burrows, Sarah, Jacinth Fairweather, Sharyn Peterson, Sharon Font, Sonya Merriel and Bonita Veal.

To my brother-in-law, Fadiga Aboubacar, Sidibe Hadja, Amy, Sidibe Zenab, and Aicha(Ohio) thank for support and believing in me.

Special thank to my friend, Hubert Daleba Gnolou. I know you been always there for me.

To my best friend, Meite Ibrahim Jean. Thank you for holding me down.

To my friends James W. Martin Jr. aka Jalike Ashanti Heru Herukhati, and Norma van Demark aka Ewunike Adesimbo.

Thanks to A & B and Culture Plus for their support and for believing in me.

Thanks to all of the readers who sampled the manuscript and gave me their feedback. There are too many of you to name individually, but you all know who you are, and I'm extremely grateful.

To my special friends from Sweden, Jaqueline Carleson, Lisa Erickson, and Haddy.

To one of my dearest brothers & friend, Sidibe Siaka, his wife, and two sons. I can't thank you enough for what you have done for me.

To my big brother, Ousmane Fofana "Restaurant bon appetit". Thank you for believing in me.

To my friend Marlon. L. 162+Jamaica do your thing.

To my friend from Burundi, Aimable Rulinda.

To Christine Jordan "28 Precinct Harlem". Thank you for keeping our community safe.

To my brother, Inza Sangare "Brikiki", and Kashan Robinson, best-selling author, of Veil of Friendship. Thank you so much for your support.

To my friends in Germany. Thank you so much for your support.

To my brother-in-law, Graig, and his beautiful wife, Corinne. Thank you for encouraging me.

To my man from Paris, Aaron Barrer, "le Congolais blanc". Grand merci. To my best friend, Ahmed Kaba "Bajo" le prince charmant de New York". Keep doing your thing.

To my friend & partner, Raphael aka Pepe, Trazar Variety Book Store, 40 Hoyt Street, Brooklyn, NY. Thank you for your support.

Special thanks to Kevin E. Young. If it weren't for you the project would not have been completed.

And a shout out to Sophie Gnoto, Saidu and Badio.

DEDICATION

I dedicate this book to
to all my readers.

PROLOGUE

Amina

As the airplane descends onto the runway at John F. Kennedy International Airport, I look to the west and see buildings bigger than any I've ever seen. They are so tall, they seem to scrape the sky.

I've dreamed about coming to America for a long time. My family has wanted one of us to come here and make a good life for ourselves. We've always heard that America is the land of opportunity, that here you can be whatever you dream of being. There's no corruption in the government. There's no constant fighting in the streets. A person can feel safe knowing that when she returns home at night, her family will be as safe and sound as when she left in the morning.

My two brothers and two sisters have not been as fortunate as I have been. I met Alou. I am so thankful. When he visited West Africa last summer, and we first looked at each

1

other, we fell in love. We just knew. He was the most beautiful man I'd ever seen. He looked powerful and confident. He wanted to marry me almost immediately. I was sixteen then. Now I am seventeen and coming to New York City to be with my man.

We were married after only a few short weeks of knowing each other. My family gave our union their blessing, as did the elders in our tribe. They all saw that not only were we in love, but Alou could give me a better life as an American citizen.

It took some time to make the arrangements so I could join him. First, he wanted to make sure that everything was perfect for me. And then I had to apply for my visitor's visa. After I settle in, we will make my U.S. citizenship official. The wait will be worth it. Even if America will not recognize our marriage because I am underage, I know that we will happily spend our lives together in the most magical place on Earth.

Alou. Chills course through my body in anticipation. I can't wait to see him again and relive all the emotions I felt when I first laid eyes on him. Oh, I cannot tell you how the sight of his rippled abdomen made my skin tingle. Or how impressed I was with his broad shoulders and thick arms. He was so gorgeous, I could barely breathe around him. And now he will be all mine, and we will build the most beautiful life together.

Alou

Amina will be landing soon. I am very nervous. This is the first time I have brought a woman from the Motherland here to New York.

My bride is very beautiful. Her face is smooth and clear, her behind is perfectly rounded, her breasts are plump and firm, and she is only sixteen years old! I am a dozen years older than her but her family didn't seem to care. In fact, I think they see the difference in our ages as a positive.

Amina and I are from the same village in West Africa. Life is so much simpler there than here. But here in the United States, the opportunities are truly endless. I came here two years ago to work with my uncle building houses. Here is Harlem, to be exact.

I wish I had known Amina when I was living on my parents' farm. Our lives would have been different. We could have been happy there. She is a very special girl. Smart as well. But she was too young for me then and we did not socialize in the same circles.

Harlem women are challenging, to say the least. It has taken me a while to get used to their sharp tongues and fast ways. I don't always like them. But I appreciate where they are coming from. They are only trying to survive, just like me. It will be a welcome break to have Amina here with me, a breath of fresh air.

I sometimes miss the respect for tradition we have back home. But it cannot be the same here. Everything is different, and I have learned how to fit into this society. I learned that if I didn't open my eyes and look past tradition, I would never accomplish a thing. I have been doing alright up until now. Amina will be my ticket to an even better life. Everything is about to change.

I borrowed my uncle's car to pick Amina up at the airport. He didn't hesitate lending me his Cadillac. He knows I like to do things in style. I'm saving up to buy an Escalade. Just a few more months.

Arrivals is busy but I find a spot at the curb. Women dressed in traditional African dress filter out the door with their luggage and children behind them. I crane my neck to get a glimpse of my bride. I can't leave the car but I know that as soon as she exits, she'll see me. She'll be so excited.

I've just stepped out of the car when a police officer approaches.

"Move along," the cop tells me.

"My wife will be out in a minute," I tell him. "There! See? She's pulling a red suitcase."

The cop doesn't turn his head to look. "Listen," he says, "you have to move your vehicle now. Park in the lot and then come back and get her."

"But, officer, she's right there!"

"I don't care. You cannot park here," he says.

I don't budge. Screw him! I stand my ground.

"License and registration, sir," he says.

"What?" I protest. "I'll be gone in a minute."

"Sir, I need to see your license and registration," he insists.

"Fine, fine, fine," I say. Maybe it'll buy me a few more minutes.

The cop heads back to his car with my documents and I can see Amina through the glass. She is asking someone for instructions. I wave but she does not see me.

The cop is back – with his partner. What now?

"Sir, please step away from the car," the officer tells me. I don't like the sound of his voice.

"Why?" I ask. "What's the problem?"

"This isn't your car," the officer replies.

"I know. I borrowed it so I could..."

"You borrowed it?" the cop asks in disbelief.

"Yes, I did. You can call my uncle if..."

"And we ran a quick check on you. You don't have a social security number."

"What? What difference does that make? I'm just about to pick up my wife and..."

"We have to confiscate this car and take you in," his partner tells me.

"But why?" I ask. "What was I doing other than being black?" I shout angrily.

"Are you saying we are harassing you because you're black?"

"I, uh, didn't mean..."

"Fraselli, cuff him!" the cop orders his partner.

"Why? What did I do?" I cry.

"You are in this country illegally and we have to take

you to INS. Right now."

"But my wife!" I scream. "She knows no one here. I have to get her!"

"Call her from INS," the partner says snidely.

I'm beside myself. I struggle to squeeze between the two officers and run to Amina who has just exited Arrivals. She sees me and a broad smile grows across her face, right before the cops grab my arms and spin me around. My face is now pressed against the hood of the car and I feel handcuffs being slipped onto my wrists.

"Why are you doing this?" I cry.

"You are resisting, that's why," the partner says. And with that, they drag me away.

"You can't detain me!" I say. My pleas fall on deaf ears. I'm in a panic. I look at Amina and her face has paled in horror. "Amina!" I scream. "Amina! Find me!!!" And with those last words, I am stuffed into the back of a patrol car and whisked away.

CHAPTER ONE

Alone

Amina

As I watch the baggage carousel go round and round, I feel my impatience growing. Where are my bags?

I'm just anxious. Alou is waiting for me and I can't wait to be with him. Nothing more than that. So I will suffer through and be patient.

Finally, my red trolley and overnight bag slip through the little door and fall onto the carousel. I watch as they creep toward me at a snail's pace.

I have trouble lifting the bigger bad and a nice gentleman assists me. I give him an appreciative smile as I extend the handle. With one bag over my shoulder and the other trailing behind me, I make my way through the crowd.

A clerk checks the numbers on my baggage claim stubs with those on my luggage. They match. I then ask directions. There are several sets of doors and I don't know which to take. Should I go upstairs? The clerk is very pleasant, if not a little abrupt, and points me in the right direction.

I feel the cool air wafting through the open door. It smells different than home, moist and fresh, like African evenings although it is mid-morning now.

I scan the crowd, searching for my husband. Then I see him. His chocolate skin almost glows. But he is not alone. He looks troubled. Then I see that he is being forcibly led away from a big white car by two men in uniform.

My smile fades as I see him struggle to break free and come to me. I hear him shout my name. I hear him say 'find me'. And I hear the door of the police car slam shut.

This is some sort of crazy mistake, I tell myself. I stand at the curb for a long time in the belief that he will return at any moment. The crowd thins. And before long, it's just me. He isn't coming back. I don't understand.

His last words echo in my mind. Find me. OK. I will find him. Where do I start?

I rummage through my backpack and pull out the stack of letters he has written to me. I take a few out and read through them. Maybe there will be some sort of clue in them. Then I realize that all I have to do is look at the return address. In block print, I find my answer. 1570 Amsterdam Avenue.

A couple of his letters mention 'Harlem'. So that is where I have to go.

I go back inside Arrivals and ask a woman behind the

information desk how I get to Harlem. She asks me if I want to be economical or take a taxicab. I choose to be economical.

A half hour later, I am on something called the AirTrain to a place called Jamaica. At Jamaica, I get instructions for finding the 'F subway'. When I'm finally on the F train, I see there is a map on the wall. After asking a fellow passenger where Harlem is, I map out the route to my desired destination. I'm on my way!

****

Once I get to Harlem…well, I have to be honest, it's not what I expected. True, there are many tall buildings and it's much more built up than my village back home. But there's trash in the streets that no one seems to be interested in cleaning up. I see a few people looking intoxicated in the middle of the day for no apparent reason. And I see a couple of grown, healthy men begging for change. What is this place? Men from my village would never do these things.

As I survey my surroundings and try to figure out which way to go, a group of men approach and start grabbing at my things.

"Oh my God! What are you doing?" I scream in both terror and confusion.

"Give me your shit, bitch, before I have to fuck you up!" one of the hoodlums snarls at me.

I can't believe it. I'm in Harlem for not even ten minutes and someone is trying to rob me.

I lock eyes with a man driving by. I'm not sure if he can see my fear but he stops. Is he going to help me? I hope so. I hope Allah has sent me a savior.

CHAPTER TWO

One Night Stand

Kevin

"Another day, another dollar," people say. I love dollars but why do we have to work so damned hard to make them?

I'm up every morning before the sun. I own two apartment buildings in Harlem, and I've also invested in a hair-braiding salon on 125th Street. I can't say that I'm fond of Salima, the crude, greedy bitch who runs the place. But as she long as she pays me, and as long as she keeps bringing in beautiful African women, I'll tolerate her. My fiancée, Lisa, is as bright as a sister could be but she could use a little more soul and a bit more dark chocolate in her.

When I step into the salon, it's like I've stepped into an exotic new world – sensual tropical fragrances, foreign languages spoken by plump lips, curvaceous hips wrapped in brightly colored fabrics. Ah. I lose myself in lust each and every time.

I love African women. I admit it. But since I proposed to Lisa, I've not let them distract me. Until recently, that is. Lisa's going through some type of phase and she's been acting differently towards me. I don't know what's up with her. We used to have wild sex, anywhere and everywhere – in a theater, in the bathroom of every restaurant we ate at, in the back seat of the car under the Manhattan Bridge, in the bushes in Central Park. Shall I continue? You get the point. All I'm trying to say is that we used to get it on.

She changed several months ago. Her freaky side turned off like a flick of a switch. I don't know why. She used to flaunt her body in front of me, stepping out of the shower dripping wet and parading around the bedroom as she dried herself off. Being naked was how she liked to be. Then one day, she asked me to leave the bedroom so she could get dressed. When I asked why, she didn't answer. Now she gets dressed IN the bathroom.

She definitely cannot be ashamed of her body. She doesn't have an ass like Buffy the Body but she has a nice little onion. She's toned from working out every morning at Gold's Gym. Women would kill to be her perfect size 6 and have natural 36C tatas. Lisa is a woman who *should* walk around the house butt naked.

Before whatever changed, Lisa was on top of things. She busted my ass about getting my daughter, Aaliyah, off to school on time and would help her get ready. She would leave with me at the crack of dawn to get to the gym before it got too crowded for her to work out. And we had freaky sex whenever we were in the mood. Now, Lisa barely moves in the morning. Where the fuck did all her energy go?

I didn't sign up for a sexless relationship with a woman who's ashamed of her body, who won't let me get physical with her, who no longer wants to have fun, and who only seems to enjoy sleeping all over the damned place.

Something is not right. Something is definitely not right with Lisa. She needs to get her shit together.

Maybe it's Michelle, her sister. Michelle's found God. She's all into the religious thing. But, no, I can't talk bad about Michelle. She's really been there for me since Lisa's been slipping. I shouldn't talk down on her. She's good to Aaliyah. But Lisa? She has to step up her game, for real. I put those two carats on her finger because of who she was – not who's trying to be now. I'm completely confused.

It's always *'Kevin do this'* and *'Kevin do that'*. I do what she asks, but then she loses her fucking mind! Somehow I'm always wrong and it's never enough. And she has one hell of a temper, too. What's with that?

Lisa had been dropping hints that we should get married for months. Maybe it was years. I don't know. But not long after I proposed, got down on one knee and gave her the ring in front of her entire family, she started to fuck up. She could have at least waited until after we walked down the aisle! Not that it would have made me feel any better. But you know what I'm saying.

So now all think about are African lips and African hips. Shit! I know, I know. I'm tripping. But what can be expected when a man's used to sexing his girl twice a day, every day for years, then the shit gets shut down?

Damn! We used to do Happy Hour a couple of times a week. We used to fuck. We used to have fun! Now all I do is work my ass off then beat my dick in the bathroom after Aaliyah goes to sleep. I don't even have to worry about Lisa. She's always sleeping. She's sleeping our relationship away.

Lisa

I love Kevin. Beyond belief. It's unreal how much I love him. He's who I want to spend my life with. But our life has become so…predictable. Not boring. Just predictable.

Everything ran like clockwork. We would fuck in the shower every morning before Aaliyah woke up. We would fuck again in some bar at night, or in the car outside of some bar, or if we couldn't find the right situation, on the couch after Aaliyah went to sleep.

Kevin is fun. A lot of fun. But he doesn't hear me when I'm talking to him. He doesn't listen.

I'll give you a for-instance. My sister is willing to watch Aaliyah every once in a while so Kevin and I can have an 'adult' night at home. I remind him all the time but he doesn't understand my need to fuck in a bed every once in a while. He doesn't get it that when it's feeling good, when he hits that exact right spot, I just want to fucking scream without worrying. I don't want to explain to Aaliyah what we're doing – as if she doesn't already know!

Kevin has swagger. He's not a cornball. He's in control. But does he have to control every fucking thing?

"Kevin can we do this?" I'd ask.

"No," he'd answer.

"Why not?" I'd ask.

"Cuz I don't want to," he'd answer.

But what about what I want? What about what anybody else might want? Just because he has a couple of dollars doesn't mean he's the boss of me.

"I pay the cost to be the boss," he always says.

"Yeah… yeah… yeah," I reply.

When I start bitching, he says, "Waaaa," as if I'm crying like a baby. I hate that fucking shit.

That's the reason why I put him on knock off. He doesn't even realize it. I won't even let him look at my ass.

I used to walk around totally naked like, "Nigga you can take this pussy any time you want it… it's yours." But not anymore. He fucked up. Now he has to get back on my good side. He has to stop stifling my voice and remember that I'm a *black* woman. I may be light-skinned but I'm still black. Tell me, what black woman is going to keep quiet just because her man says so? Exactly! That's my point. He's been taking me for granted, and I have to remind him of what he's in jeopardy of losing.

Why is it when you've finally met the one man you know will be there for you, and when you know in your heart that he just needs to adjust a tiny bit to work out the kinks in the relationship, another nigga comes along? Why is it when you're angry, you lose focus and momentarily forget that in this world of losers, you have one of the winners? I don't know but it seems to happen every time.

Back in the day, I used to have a huge crush on Malik. He's a hustler, and I said I would never mess with a hustler, but Malik was so…delicious. He invented the word swagger. For real. Women didn't always say yes to Malik like they do with Kevin. Then Malik didn't always ask. And if he did, women would yes because they were afraid he'd kick their asses if they didn't. Malik's type of power is sexy as hell.

Malik wasn't good for me, though. He got me started sniffing coke. I never told Kevin. For a while, I was really fucked up. My habit got so bad I went into a rehab program upstate to get clean.

So why in the hell did I have to run into Malik's sexy ass now? And why have I allowed myself to get caught up again in the same bullshit as before?

All Malik had to do was say, "Hey, shorty," and look at me with those piercing eyes of his. Next thing I knew, I was riding with him to the Bronx.

Yes. Yes. It felt good to get dicked down in a real bed. It felt good to moan and scream in passion when he hit the spot. And goddamn, did Malik ever hit the spot! Like always.

Not that Kevin misses all the time. I'd say he's batting 800. But with Malik batting 1000, what in the world is a sister supposed to do?

So I've been letting him tax this ass ever since. But I don't love him. I love my fiancé. I love Kevin. He's who I'm going to be with. I hate what I'm doing to him. I just have to get over this thing with Malik. I have to relinquish the power he has over me. I have to be tough and stick to my...

"Hello?...Hey Malik...you're where...for real?...I'll be right over."

Shit.

So much for taking control. He's next door at my neighbor's house. Good. I'm not gonna do anything I'll regret with Aaliyah right the fuck next door! I can control myself for ten minutes. I'll stand up for myself and not fuck up my life again. Fate may have intervened at both the exact right and wrong times. At least this time I know whcih end is up.

"What up, shorty?" Malik asks before he shoves his tongue into my mouth.

I don't want to kiss him, I tell myself, but I accept his kiss nonetheless. Hell, I even kiss him back.

"Malik...we have to talk," I gasp after I push away from him.

"About what?" he asks. "I don't have a lot of time. I have to check out some shit in the Bronx. Besides, I brought that powder you like. You know how it takes you there when you're pumping on this." Malik has been unbuttoning his jeans this whole time. Now he whips out his semi-hard dick and swings it around.

"Where's Andre?" I ask.

"Running an errand for me," Malik tells me. "We have the place to ourselves for an hour."

"Shit!" I snap. "Kevin will be home early today. I didn't come over here expecting this. I came over here to talk."

"Stop the bullshit and get over here," Malik orders.

As if I'm in a trance, I oblige him. Not even a minute later I'm kneeling down in front of Malik. Two minutes after snorting my line of coke, Malik's dick is in my mouth and I'm making him squirm. Ten minutes later, his dick is inside of me and he's making me squirm.

Way to have a talk and stand up for myself, I say to myself as I leave Andre's house with my soggy, dumb, whorish ass.

"Lisa! What the fuck are you doing?" Kevin asks as he slams his car door. His angry eyes bore into my guilty ones. "What were you doing over there? And who in the hell is watching Aaliyah?"

Damn, this is all the fuck I need, I think to myself. *This is all I fucking need.*

CHAPTER THREE

Welcome to Harlem

Kevin

"Bitch! Who the fuck is watching my daughter?" I holler, seething.

"You will not talk to me like that!" Lisa screams. "I am not your bitch! I'm nobody's bitch!"

"If you're not a bitch than stop acting like one," I reply. "Look at your fucking hair! Now I understand why you ain't been giving me none lately. Who you been fucking, Lisa? Who do you know in that building? If you're nobody's bitch, you sure are acting like a straight ho. I can't believe your fucking ass!"

"Stop disrespecting me!" Lisa snaps.

"Stop disrespecting you?" I reply. "You disrespected yourself. Make me fucking ask you again who's watching my daughter!"

"She's watching TV...she's fine," Lisa says. "I just had

to take care of something for a second."

"Take care of something? What the hell do you have to take care of in that building that made you to leave my daughter by herself?"

"I told you she's fine," Lisa says.

"I hear you talking but so far you ain't said shit!" I say angrily. "Who do you know in there, Lisa?"

Lisa remains quiet.

"Answer me."

Silence.

"You know what? Since you ain't got shit to say you can tell your story walking."

"What do you mean?" Lisa asks.

"Get the fuck out of my house!" I snap. "And I mean tonight."

"Stop tripping," Lisa says. "Kevin, you're overreacting."

"Call it whatever you want but get your shit and get out," I holler.

"Yeah right," Lisa replies casually.

I grab her forcefully by the shoulders and push her up against the door.

"I'm not fucking playing with you, Lisa," I say stoically. "Take your shit and get the fuck out of here. Tonight. And don't try to make a scene in front of Aaliyah or it's gonna be a problem."

"Wow…you're serious," Lisa says.

"As a heart attack," I say.

"You're tripping," Lisa says casually like it's a joke. "But if that's what you want then that's what you'll get. I won't bother Aaliyah at all."

Lisa follows me into the house and starts to quietly pack her things. I hear her softly whimpering, and I hope she's hurting. I can't believe she would play me out after all I've done for her.

"I want you to know that you're making a terrible mistake," Lisa says. "What am I supposed to tell my mom when I go there tonight? You know how much she loves you and Aaliyah."

"Tell her the truth. Tell her what you wouldn't tell me. Tell her where you were and what you were doing when you left my daughter unsupervised in the house," I say.

"Whatever," Lisa says.

I see that she's trying to act cocky and be brave but her eyes are telling me that she's torn apart. I truly hope she's hurting as badly as the thought of her with another man is hurting me.

She drags her feet to the door. Part of me wants to demand she give back my keys. But asking for them would cause a conversation and I'm not in the mood for more lies. I don't want her yelling at me, not saying shit. And I don't want her to tear me down. Right now, I just want her ass gone. I need to stick to my guns. She's changed and I need to know why. She needs to know that she's losing me and can't keep doing whatever it is she's doing, thinking that everything is gonna be cool with me. Treat me the way I deserve to be treated – the way she used to treat me – or don't come back.

****

I wake up to Aaliyah shaking my leg. To my surprise, I spent the night on the sofa.

"OK, baby. Finish getting yourself together and I'll take you to school," I say.

"Dad, I'm already dressed!" Aaliyah says. "We have to go now!"

I groggily crack open my eyes and lift my arm to look at my watch.

"Oh no! You're about to be late," I say. "Did you eat?"

"Yes, sir," she responds. "I ate some cereal."

I love how polite she is.

"Baby, you don't even like cereal," I say. "I'm sorry."

"That's okay, Daddy," Aaliyah says. "You looked like you needed to sleep."

My baby is so sweet. I love her to pieces.

****

As I drive Aaliyah to school, I remember the crazy dream I had last night. I had called Joey Greco and Cheaters and asked them to follow Lisa. Since I wasn't trying to hear her bullshit and was frustrated that she hadn't told me anything, I didn't want to deal with her.

In the dream, the guys found her and the dude she's

been fucking with. I whipped his ass then started beating her down. I grabbed her by the hair and punched her hard in the face.

Remembering the dream weirds me out. I don't get down like that. Any man who beats on a woman is a punk-ass bitch. I'm mad at Lisa, and I want her to be hurting, but I don't understand the point of my dream. I'm not the type of dude to beat a woman.

＊＊＊＊

After I drop Aaliyah off at school, I take a drive so I can think about my situation. I snap out of my thoughts when I pass a group of three thugs trying to rob what appears to be my African dream girl. I don't particularly feel the need to risk my own safety, but I can't drive by and pretend that I don't see what's happening.

Maybe I'm feeling guilty about my dream of punching Lisa in the face. I'm not sure. But I stop the car and run to the defenseless African girl's aid.

"Stop! What the fuck are you doing?" I scream.

"Mind your business!" one of the thugs hollers back at me.

"My mind is my business," I say as I grab his fingers and pull them off her bag. "Leave her alone! Go and try to take some shit from a man your own size!" I say as I push him away.

"Bitch, you may be bigger than me but it's three of us

and one of you," the thug threatens.

"Well then, let's get it popping," I say. "If you feel froggy then leap, motherfucker."

The thug lunges at me, and I punch him squarely in the face. He falls to the ground, right on his ass.

That appears to be enough to scare his two accomplices away. They take off, running in opposite directions.

"Thank you so much," the African beauty says.

"Are you alright?" I ask. "They didn't hurt you, did they?"

"No...you got here just in time," she says with a grateful smile.

"What's your name?" I ask.

"Oh," she replies as she bends down to gather her things. "My name is Amina. What's yours?"

"My name is Kevin," I say. "Amina, let me help you." We take a few moments to repack her things. "Where were you headed before they attacked you?"

"Well...wow. This is embarrassing," Amina says.

"Why do you say that?" I ask. "I won't judge you."

"Actually, I don't know exactly where I'm going. Here," she says as she reaches into her bag. "I'm trying to find this address." She shows me an envelope with a return address on Amsterdam.

"I know where this is," I tell her. "Can I take you there if you want."

Amina thinks it over. "That would be so kind of you. Thank you," she says and starts to cry.

"Aw, sweetheart, don't cry," I say. "I'll take you there. Not a problem."

"You are so kind to help me. Today has been such an awful day," she says.

"I can certainly understand why you would be so upset. Those thugs were about to take all your things."

"It's not just that, Kevin," she says as she wipes at her eyes. "My husband was supposed to pick me up at the airport and I don't have anyone here but him. I don't know anyone here but him. If I don't find him, I don't know what I'm going to do."

Amina starts to cry all over again.

A part of me is disappointed that she's married. She's cute as shit.

"Hey, it's not that bad. Now you know me. And I'm not going to leave you all alone here in Harlem," I say. "Consider me your first new friend in America."

Amina looks at me gratefully and flashes a bright smile.

"See, that's better," I say. "Your smile is breathtaking. You're very beautiful. For the rest of the day, I'm going to try to make smile."

"I hope I don't let you down," Amina says, again showing her glistening white teeth and deep dimples.

"God, you're beautiful," I say. "How old are you?"

"I just turned seventeen," Amina replies. "Alou and I are going to celebrate my birthday."

"Alou?"

"I'm sorry," Amina replies. "Alou is my husband. That's

who I'm trying to find."

"How old is Alou?" I ask.

"Why? Would you know him?" Amina asks.

"No, I don't know think so. I'm just curious for other reasons," I say. "American laws are different from African laws."

"Different?" Amina asks, inquisitively. "How do you mean?"

"In this country, you have to be seventeen in order to consent to be with a grown man," I say. "If you're not seventeen and a man is with you intimately, he can be charged with statutory rape. That is one of this country's most serious crimes, punishable by years in prison. Inmates don't treat offenders of statutory rape kindly."

"Oh. Alou is twenty-eight but greatly respected in my village," Amina says. "My parents were not concerned about his age."

"Well, not to speak badly about your parents, but I wish they would have been concerned," I say. "He's old enough to be your young uncle. Hell, in this country with so many kids having kids, he's almost old enough to be your father."

"Eeeeww…that's sick," Amina says.

"That's exactly what I'm saying," I tell Amina. "In this country, we think it's very sick for older men to be involved with teenagers who are not yet of legal age."

"But he's the only man I know in this country. Besides you," Amina says. "And no matter what you might say or think, I'm in love with him."

Amina looks sad so I change the subject.

"Let's go try to find him then," I say as I carry her bags to my car.

When we pull up to Alou's apartment building, a group of men is standing by the entrance. I immediately recognize one of them.

"Uh oh. I think this is bad news, Amina."

"Bad news? Why bad news?" she asks.

"Well, I invested in a hair braiding salon not far from here," I say. "There are quite a few African girls working for me. Many of them are here illegally. That guy over there, the tall one with the gray hair? He works for INS. And since he's here, it means Alou is in trouble."

"INS?" Amina asks.

"The Immigration and Naturalization Service," I explain. "Its purpose is to make sure that people aren't in this country illegally. Mainly, they try to remove foreigners. If INS is here, they're conducting an investigation. They may be looking for you too."

"Are you joking right now?" Amina asks.

"I wish I was," I say. "I wish I was."

CHAPTER FOUR

Kevin, My Savior

Amina

The shock is too much. I don't know what else to do but cry so I cry my eyes out as Kevin drives me to safety.

I don't know where we are going but at least I'm content to be with someone who has been kind to me in this foreign place.

I wonder what my father would say if he knew what was happening. What would he do to Alou? Alou apparently misled everyone in the village. He told us that he was an American citizen. We were married according to the customs of our tribe. I gave myself to him! I am in shock. I am shaking. Why would Alou lie to me? And what will happen to me now?

"Where are we going?" I ask Kevin. "It seems like we're riding in circles."

"We have been," he confesses. "I didn't know what to

do. You haven't been able to talk."

"I'm sorry," I tell him. "I think I'm done crying for now."

"For now?"

"Yes, for now," I say sadly. "Give me a break. I've had a really hard day."

"True, true," I reply. "Are you hungry?"

"I'm famished," Amina says.

Cute and a good vocabulary, too, I say to myself. Then to Amina, "I'd better feed you then before some other man tries to steal you from me," Kevin says.

I laugh with my voice but not with my eyes. It may be a long time before I will.

Kevin

I take Amina to one of my favorite African restaurants, one Lisa doesn't know about. I have no idea what I'm going to do but I don't need her blowing up my spot while I'm trying to figure it out.

Amina scarfs down everything on her plate and then eats some of what's on mine. She appears to be more relaxed now so I figure it's a good time to talk.

"What are you going to do?" I ask.

"I have absolutely no idea," Amina responds with a sad laugh.

"At least you can laugh about it," I say.

"I'm worn out from crying," Amina says. "I'm laughing only so I don't start crying again."

"I'd offer that you stay with me but I don't know how you'd feel about it. My life is kind of complicated."

"You're married," Amina says. "You live with your wife in one of these beautiful houses."

"No, no. I'm not married. I live with my daughter. I don't have a wife." Of course I don't tell Amina the entire story.

"Where is your daughter's mother?" Amina asks.

"She died giving birth to Aaliyah," I tell her.

"I'm so sorry, Kevin," Amina says sincerely. "How old is your daughter?"

"She just turned seven," I say.

"You've been raising her all alone?" she asks.

"Well, I've had help," I say and leave it at that. "I love my daughter very much," I say. "We have each other and that's the most important thing." Now is not the time to explain my current drama. Knowing Lisa and her stubborn ass, I'm sure Amina will find out soon enough.

"So, you didn't answer about staying with me," I say. "Is it a go or a no go?"

"I guess it's a go," Amina says. "I hate to be repetitive with the word go and redundant about my situation but I have nowhere else *to* go."

I smile. "Pretty girl with a big vocabulary," I say. "My daughter will love you. You can help her with her homework."

After I pay the bill and we head to the car, I feel strangely relieved to know that, at least temporarily, she'll be staying in my home. I feel very concerned about her well-being.

****

"Daddy, Daddy! Lisa is back!" Aaliyah shouts when I open the door.

She jumps into my arms, almost knocking me down.

"Why didn't you wait for me?" I ask. "I was only a couple minutes late. I don't want you to leave school alone. Any crazy person can snatch you while…"

"But I didn't, Daddy," Aaliyah interrupts. "Lisa picked me up. I told you that Lisa is back."

"Yes, baby, I came back to apologize," I hear Lisa say behind me. "I'm so sorry about last night. I don't like the way things went down…" She stops mid-sentence when she notices Amina standing by the front door. "Umm, Kevin, who is this?"

"Who?" I stammer.

"Who else, Kevin?" Lisa snaps. "Her. This girl here. Damn, I'm not even gone one full day and you've robbed the cradle!"

"Lisa, it's not like that," I say. "And who are you to say anything to me after the way you've been acting lately? You left me hanging with too many unanswered questions to be asking me anything!"

31

"Well, if it's not like that then who is she? And why does she have luggage with her?" Lisa asks.

"Wait just one minute. We're not going to do this in front of my daughter," I say before turning to Aaliyah. "Aaliyah, go to your room."

"But Dad…" Aaliyah protests.

"Go to your room now!" I snap.

"Yes sir," Aaliyah says before sulking away.

"I thought you said you didn't live with anyone," Amina whispers to me but Lisa hears.

"No, that's not what I said," I whisper back. "You asked if I lived with my wife and I said I didn't…"

"Well, you implied that you didn't live with anyone," Amina says, cutting me off.

"I only live with my daughter," I say. "I didn't imply anything. I don't have anything to imply."

"See, I knew you wasn't all up in those African bitches' faces for nothing," Lisa says. "You just had to go get yourself one."

"Watch your mouth," I say. "I don't have to explain anything to you. You never answer any of my questions. Besides, I already told you it's not like that. Amina has had a rough enough day, and I'm not going to allow you to insult her under my roof."

"Oh, so her name is Amina?" Lisa says. "Amina, I'm Lisa." Lisa extends her hand to Amina. "His fiancée."

"Fiancée? Does that mean the two of you are engaged to be married?" Amina asks.

"Yes, we are very fucking engaged," Lisa says sarcastically.

"We're engaged?" I say. " We were engaged, Lisa. Stop pretending that last night didn't happen."

"The operative phrase you just used was last night...*last night*, Kevin," Lisa says angrily. "We had an argument last night, Kevin. I left last night, Kevin. And I didn't take all of my stuff last night, Kevin. Now, today, you're trying to move this bitch in when our disagreement was just *last night*? You don't waste any time, do you?"

"Stop acting like you're the victim, Lisa," I say. "And I asked you not to call her names."

"You're mighty protective of this Amina person," Lisa says. "How long you been fucking her?"

"I really don't have anything to do with this," Amina says uncomfortably. "Maybe I should leave."

"You don't have to answer to her, Amina," I say. "And Lisa, you're straight tripping. You're asking all of these questions like everything is still everything and you still haven't answered my simple questions from last night. Whose house were you coming from and why was it so important for you to leave Aaliyah alone while you were doing whatever?"

"Don't try to change the subject, Kevin," Lisa says.

"No. You've been trying to change the subject, Lisa," I say. "I keep asking and asking but you don't answer. Well, I have another question. Is the reason you haven't been giving me none lately because you've been fucking someone else?"

"Now you're really tripping," Lisa says.

"When was the last time you let me touch you? When was the last time you even let me look at your naked ass? So who's tripping?"

"Kevin," Lisa says with a huge sigh, "You've been taking me for granted. I had to put you on knock off to make a point."

"Oh, so all of this is somehow my fault?"

"Kevin, look," Lisa says. "I didn't come here to argue with you. I came here to make up with you. Yes, I have been distant lately but that's only because I was mad at you. I was talking to you and I felt like you weren't listening..."

"There you go, blaming me again," I interrupt.

"Baby, please!" Lisa says. "I'm not blaming everything on you. I accept my responsibility for what happened. I just need for you to know that I love you. I really, really, REALLY love you. That's why I'm here. I wanted you to know how I feel before things went too far off course. Now, I have no idea why this woman is here, and I'm sorry for accusing you but you have to know how this looks."

"Baby, I told you it's not what it looks like," I say. "It's not what you think."

"That's good to know and thank you, thank you for calling me baby," Lisa says as she grabs my hand. "That means you still love me, I hope."

She pulls me close to her and kisses me softly.

"I love you, baby, and I don't want to lose you," Lisa

says. "Now please tell me who this is."

"Amina?" I say even though it's obvious.

"Kevin, I love you but please don't make me crack you upside your fucking head," Lisa says angrily.

"Amina is nobody," I say then correcting myself. "I'm sorry, Amina. I don't mean to say that you're a nobody. I'm just saying that you're not what Lisa thinks you are."

"I already told her that I don't have anything to do with this," Amina says.

"Why thank you, Amina," Lisa says sarcastically before turning to me. "OK, so if it's not what I think then what is it?"

"Amina is going to be staying here with me for a while until she can figure some things out," I say matter-of-factly.

"Excuse me? Staying with *you*?" Lisa asks. "I'm sure you meant to say staying with us. You did mean to say staying with *us*, right?"

"She has nothing to do with what happened last night," I say. "She has nothing to do with what's going on between us."

"True that," Lisa says. "She doesn't. And since you're so calm, I believe you. But...and this is a very big but...irregardless of what happened last night, or any other night, if you think you're going to move some bitch in here after putting me out and I'm gonna be cool with it, you've lost your fucking mind! I love you, but I'm not dumb. Do you think I'm dumb, Kevin?"

"Nobody said you were dumb, Lisa," I say.

"Good. I'm glad that's documented – that I'm not fucking stupid," Lisa says. "That makes me feel a lot better." She turns to Amina. "Now, Miss Amina, you can stay here with *us*." She looks at me as she emphasizes the word us. "But before you unpack, someone is going to tell me what the hell is going on!"

"No disrespect, Miss Lisa," Amina says. "But it's not my place to explain things to you. If the two of you are engaged to be married as you say, I, as another woman, should not be speaking for him."

"At least you didn't pick a dumb one, Kevin," Lisa says.

"Listen, Lisa. Stop!" I say, exasperated. "It just so happens that after I dropped Aaliyah off at school, I was driving to work and spotted three dudes trying to rob Amina. I just couldn't sit there and let it happen. So I chased the guys away and helped her with her things. That's when she told me her name and where she was headed. Her husband was supposed to have picked her up from the airport this morning but he didn't show. So I gave her a ride to his place and we saw INS guys hanging outside her husband's apartment building.

"This is her first day in America. She doesn't know anybody else here and it looks like her husband's in trouble with INS. We don't know for sure. But I do know that it's a damned shame that all this stuff happened to her on her first day in New York. So I offered her a place to sleep until we figure out what to do."

"Damn...that's really sad," Lisa says, pretending to be

concerned. "And I've been so mean to both of you." She grabs Amina's hand. "I'm sorry, sweetie."

"That's OK," Amina says. "You have the right to want to know why another woman is in your fiancé's presence."

"Well, let's get you settled in," Lisa says. She grabs two of Amina's bags and walks with her upstairs.

I'm sure Lisa's being insincere. But knowing her, she'll play it cool so she can keep tabs on Amina. Lisa always talks about keeping friends close and enemies even closer.

But truthfully, I'm glad things went down the way they did. And I know that tonight Lisa is gonna fuck the shit out of me. She's so predictable. Who knows what tomorrow will bring? I'd better enjoy tonight.

And I don't mind having two beautiful ladies in my house. What sane man would?

I can only imagine the rumors that are going to spread about me laying up with two women. Ha! Well, all I can think to say is, "Thank you, God, for hooking me up like this!"

CHAPTER FIVE

Rules and Regulations

Kevin

"Oh my God, Lisa...Oh my God!" I holler.

Normally, I'm very quiet when we have sex in the morning because I don't want to risk waking Aaliyah. But this morning I can't help myself. I can't remember when Lisa has given it to me this good before. Saying she made my toes curl is an understatement.

"What's gotten into you?" I gasp after I climax.

"I just want you to remember how your bread is buttered," Lisa says. "There may be another woman in the house now, but I'm your woman. I can't have you forgetting that, now can I?"

"Amina is no woman. She's just a girl," I respond.

"So?" Lisa says. "She still looks hot in the ass."

"Lisa, stop it," I say. "You're still talking about a child."

"Child, my ass!" Lisa says in disgust. "She looks more of

a woman than most women I know. That's why I'll be keeping my eye on her – my third eye and everything."

"You're being ridiculous," I tell her. "Are you tripping
because you think she's more of a woman than you?"

"Bite your fucking tongue!" Lisa says after she smacks
me hard in the face. "You'd better stop disrespecting me."

"Damn, Lisa! I was just joking," I reply while rubbing
my cheek.

"Since when did I start being a joke?" Lisa asks angrily.

"I didn't say you were a joke. I said that I was joking
with you," I try to reason with her.

"That's why I can't win!" Lisa says. "I give it to your ass
good. Didn't I give it to your ass good?" I remain silent.
"Answer me!"

"Babe, you were great," I reply.

"Don't interrupt me when I'm trying to make a point!"
Lisa snaps.

"But you just told me to answer you," I say with a gig-
gle.

"You do think I'm a fucking joke!" Lisa snarls. "That's
why you keep playing games with me. Mmm hmm. I feel
you, though. I get where you're coming from. I try to
break your ass something proper and this is the thanks I get.
Now you'd better not have shit to say about why don't we
do it the way we used to. I fuck the shit out of you the way
you like and here's the thanks that I get. I can't win. You
just proved that I can't fucking win."

"Babe, you're making a big deal out of nothing," I say.

"I appreciate how you woke me up this morning. You've made me very happy." I open my arms. "I love you, baby. Please just give me a hug and peace things up."

Lisa hugs me but I'm not sure about her disposition. She still smells of attitude.

Unfortunately, I have to get up and get ready to start my day. Lisa is just going to have to work through her insecurities on her own.

Lisa

Kevin thinks he's so slick, I think while I hold onto his warm body for the last few moments before he gets out of bed. *But I have something for his ass. Whether he knows it or not, he won't be playing me out like he thinks he is.*

* * * *

I feign sleep until Kevin leaves. But no sooner than I hear the door close, I jump out of bed in a fury, grabbing my robe and slinging it over my shoulders like a prizefighter headed toward the ring.

I stomp down the stairs and stand over Amina. "Mina… Mina… Mina!" I shout at the top of my lungs. "Get that ass up! You have lots to do today."

"Good morning," Amina says with sleepy eyes. "What things?" she asks.

"Good morning, yourself!" I snap back. "And don't be fucking asking me any questions. Are you trying to get smart with me?"

"No, of course not," Amina says. "I'm just excited to hear what things we'll be doing today, that's all."

"Well, you'd better not be trying to get smart with me," I say. "For that there will be consequences and repercussions. Anyway, get up so you can get Aaliyah ready for school. But first, let me show you the house."

I show Amina around the house.

"This is where the washer and dryer are," I say. "Have you used a washer and dryer before?" Amina shakes her head no so I briefly explain how it works then continue with my laundry room rules. "Don't wash little loads of clothes. Separate the clothes into whites, dark colors, and light colors, then make sure there's enough of one set of colors to fill the washer three quarters of the way before you run it. We can't have you wasting money on electricity and water. Money doesn't grow on trees around here.

"You need to sweep and mop the kitchen floor at least once a day and vacuum the floor every other day," I tell her. "And see this phone? You are not allowed to use it. We are not going to be pay for your long distance calls to Hunga Bonga.

"I keep all the spices and seasonings in this cabinet. And that cabinet is for canned goods," I open and close doors as I explain. "We don't like food with no taste around here so season your food right when you cook. You need to get up early enough to get Aaliyah dressed and fed before school. You can make her oatmeal, Cream of Wheat, or even fry her bacon and eggs. Don't make too many eggs because the girl is a little feeble with them when it comes to using a fork. But she loves bacon. She's definitely a meat eater. And don't let her drink too much Kool-Aid no matter how much she whines. She can have one little glass of orange juice at breakfast but I prefer she drinks water. It's better for her.

"You need to sweep and mop the stairs, too," I tell Amina as we reach the top of the stairs. "This bathroom should be spic and span. There's Pine Sol under the sink, Windex for the mirror and shower door, and Tilex for the tub. This room next to the bathroom is Aaliyah's. Every morning when you return from taking her to school you need to make her bed and straighten up her toys. Oh yeah, make sure you put her clothes from the previous day in the hamper that's in the hallway closet. That hamper should be emptied on a regular basis and the clothes taken down to the basement where you'll sort them like I told you."

Amina seems like she's not concentrating so I step to her. "Let me find out you're not paying attention to me!" I say, annoyed. "It seems like you're someplace else and not here. You need to be right fucking here."

I wave my hands around in the air to emphasize my point.

"I'm sorry," Amina says. "It's just overwhelming. It's a lot for me to remember."

"Your ass had better not be slow," I say with a smirk. "But I don't care if you are. You just better remember everything I'm telling you so. Now where was I? Oh, yeah. Other than when you wake Aaliyah up and are cleaning, you are to stay out of her room. You can never sleep with her. Your place is on the couch."

"The couch hurts my back a little bit," Amina protests. "It's hard for me to get comfortable."

"Well, I have a cardboard box and a raggedy blanket for you if you prefer," I say sarcastically. "You can sleep on the sidewalk with the rest of the homeless and see how you like it."

"Don't you want me to be comfortable if I'm going to be doing all the things you ask of me?" Amina asks.

"You, comfortable? Fuck you!" I respond.

"Lisa, please…the language," Amina responds. "I'm not used to hearing foul language. Please relax. I'll be fine on the couch. What kind of an allowance will I be getting."

"From where I'm standing, a place for you to lay your head at night away from all the crazies out there on the street is all the allowance you need," I say matter-of-factly. "As I said, I have a cardboard box and raggedy blanket for you to go out there with if you don't like how things are going down in here. Believe me, there are tons of homeless people out there who would love to be in your shoes. You need to stop fucking bitching and moaning and accept the fact that I'm doing your ass a favor. And here you go talking about a fucking allowance! You must have bumped your fucking head. The only money you're going to get is money to go shopping occasionally. And you'd better show me each and every receipt to prove that you're not stealing a dime."

"Lisa, I'm not a thief," Amina protests.

"I don't know what the fuck you are," I respond. "But one thing I do know is that I'm not going to have your ass around here having free range with shit. This is not your fucking house. This is our house. And you are not to do anything around here without my permission. If a thought comes into your head and it's something I didn't already tell you to do, you'd better press the pause button. Don't fucking play with me. I don't even want your ass breathing unless I tell you to."

I push Amina against the wall when I see her take some breaths.

"I'm not fucking playing with you," I snap. "I didn't tell your ass to breath."

"I thought you were joking," Amina says. "I have to breath in order to live."

"You'll never have to worry about me joking around with you because I'm no joke," I say. "But it is OK for you to breath. The last thing I need is for you to end up dying because I told you not to breath. Then the cops would come around and you'd be fucking up our good life even though you're dead. Then you'd win. There's no way in hell I'm going to let you win."

I scratch my head and try to think if there's anything

that I'm forgetting. I give up when nothing comes to mind.

"That's all for now," I say. "You need to wake Aaliyah up and get started before she's late for school. She can never be late for school. That would be a fuck up on your part and we can't have you fucking up. I hope you paid attention or else something is gonna come back and bite you in the ass."

"Do you need my help with any of the things you have to do after I finish with Aaliyah?" Amina asks.

"Don't you fucking worry about what I'm doing or what I have to do," I say snidely. "The only thing I have to do right now is make sure that you do what you're supposed to do. Consider me your supervisor. And I'll be watching your ass to make sure you do everything right. How about that?"

Amina doesn't answer me. She just looks at me like I'm crazy. I just roll my eyes at her and stomp away. "I'll be watching you!" I shout as I go.

I know for a fact that I'm gonna have to be all over her ass like white on rice. I don't trust Amina as far as I can see her with her African, man-stealing ass.

I know for a fact that she's sneaky. I know she's up to something. Her ass had better not play with me, though. That would not be a good look for her. I very seriously doubt she could deal with my consequences and repercussions.

I hope she was listening, not only to my words but also the to tone of my voice. Lisa is not one to be played with.

Play with me and you'll end up getting played the fuck out.

CHAPTER SIX

Indentured Slavery

Amina

"See you later, Aaliyah. I'll be picking you up after school," I tell Kevin's adorable little girl.

"What about Lisa?" she asks.

I don't know how to tell her that Lisa is no longer interested in her so I tell her the truth. "Lisa has put me in charge of taking care of you in the morning and for picking you up at the end of the day. Is that alright with you?"

Aaliyah looks a little confused. "She told you to?"

"Yes, she did," I respond. "But don't worry. I will never be late. You can count on me."

This seems to put her little mind at rest. "OK, Miss Amina. I'll see you later!" she chirps and runs happily into the school.

I watch as she joins her friends and disappears inside. I hope I can remember my way back home.

Home. Whose home? Kevin owns the building but from what I can see, Lisa has claimed it as her own. I sit on a bench across the street from the school for a minute so I can think.

I don't like Lisa. Not one bit. And I don't understand why she is so angry at me. She has a good man in Kevin yet she does not really appreciate him. If she did, she would see how kind and generous he is by taking me in and giving me shelter. If she was secure in their relationship, she would have no need to be suspicious and upset about me. And if she had listened to Kevin, she would know that I am a married woman and need to find my husband. She should happily allow me to use the telephone so I can make other arrangements.

But instead, she has decided to treat me like a slave.

I find it ironic that, as a black woman, she would make me into what American black women hate most. It seems that Lisa has forgotten her history lessons. But as I saw this morning, I think she bends the rules every chance she gets to take advantage of the power she thinks she has. She thinks she is entitled to be mean to me because she will marry Kevin.

I can't tell Kevin how rude and arrogant she was. For all I know, he could have asked her to make me their slave. It is reasonable for me to have some responsibilities to pay my way. But I can't believe that Kevin would rescue me just to abuse me this way. I think Lisa is acting on her own. Still, I can't get in the middle of their relationship. I can't complain to Kevin. He will think I am interfering where I should not.

I know I have to get back to the house and figure out how to use the washing machine but all I want to do is sit here and enjoy a few moments of peace and quiet. The past few days have been grueling on me both mentlly and physically.

What has happened to Alou? That is the big question. I saw him being led away by the police. Where would they have taken him and can I go to that place? How do I find out if he has been deported? Should I call my father?

No, I can't call my father. I am so embarrassed. My family knows how much I love Alou. They all gave us their blessing. What if Alou is innocent? What if I tell my father something that is untrue? I cannot ruin his reputation in our village simply because I have jumped to a conclusion.

No, I cannot tell my father. But I can rely on him. What would he say to me right now? Be strong, be smart. Don't drown in your troubles. Pick yourself up and do what you have to do to survive. Remember that I raised you to be strong, resourceful and proud. Take the initiative and do for yourself. My father would not want me crying over a situation I am in. He would want me to find a solution to change it.

I've been sitting too long but I feel good about taking the time for myself. The street is very quiet now that the children are in class and the parents have gone to work. It's just me, someone walking his dog, and a couple of cars now.

I'd better get going. I hope I don't forget the way.

Lisa had given me the key to let myself back in. I guess that means she won't be home when I return. Good.

As I turn to cross the street, a police car cruises past me and another car makes a u-turn just after it passes. I remember to look back the other way one more time. Even though the street has quieted, I have to be careful. Harlem is not at all like my small village.

CHAPTER SEVEN

Hair Braiding Salon

Kevin

"Hi, Kevin," Amina says. "What are you doing home in the middle of the day?"

"I wanted to discuss something with you," I say. It's been two weeks since Amina arrived but she seems to already have my routine down. I see that she is a little surprised.

"What is it?" Amina asks.

"Well, you don't act like other women I know," I say. "You're different." Amina looks a little hurt. "No, no, no. I don't mean that in a bad way. It's a good thing. I mean to say that you're a different type of woman – in a good way. Does it have something to do with you being from Africa? That's what I want to know. Are you taught to be respectful? I can't put my finger on it, but I just know that you're different from all the women I've known my whole life."

"You're right, Kevin," Amina says. "The women here are much different than the women at home. African women are taught to live by a higher standard. We would never behave the way American women behave."

"That's what confuses me," I say. "The woman managing my hair salon is from Africa. In fact, most of the girls working for me braiding hair are from Africa."

"That's nice," Amina says. "You are such a special man, looking out for people who come here from the Motherland."

"I try. But Salima makes it hard for me at times," I say.

"Who is Salima?" Amina asks.

"Salima…she's who I'm talking about," I respond. "She's the manager of my hair braiding salon. She's from Africa. But she isn't anything like you. But she's been here a long time. Maybe she used to be more like you. I don't remember. But as far as now goes, Salima is as Americanized a woman as she could be. I wish she was more like you."

"Aw…thank you, Kevin," Amina replies. "I'm just being myself. It's good to know I'm appreciated, though."

"You don't know the half of it," I admit. "Aaliyah is happier than I've ever seen her. You have a good effect on people. You can turn the angriest person in the world happy."

"I wish I could make Lisa happy," Amina says. "She always seems to be mad at me."

"Well, don't worry about trying to change the way Lisa is," I say. "Let me worry about that. But I would like you to become friends with Salima and see if some of your good nature rubs off on her. I'm not so sure the salon can continue to be successful if she continues to behave the way she does."

"I'd love to meet some people from Africa!" Amina says with enthusiasm. "I'd especially like to meet other African women. What seems to be the problem with Salima?"

"Well, she's been acting differently since she had her husband arrested," I say.

"She had him arrested?" Amina asks.

"She had to," I tell her. "He was very abusive. Several times she came into the salon with bruises. I'm sure he hurt her. But still, she didn't have to turn into the victim and start acting out and making excuses for her life afterwards. Her husband is locked up so he can't hurt her anymore. She has a good job, a nice place to stay, and she got her green card. If you ask me, she has nothing to worry about. I just don't understand her."

"What is she doing?" Amina asks.

"Let me explain how I run the salon so you'll understand," I say. "I have six stylists in addition to Salima. Stylists, except for Salima because she's the manager, are supposed to pay me $100 a week to rent a chair. After that, they're supposed to pay me a twenty percent commission on each of their appointments. For the life of me, I can't understand why I'm barely clearing a thousand bucks a week because whenever I go into the shop, no matter which day, it's packed. It just doesn't add up. I think Salima's skimming off the top though I can't prove it."

"Do you really think she'd do that?" Amina asks. "The African women I know have better values than that."

"Values?" I ask. "Would you like to know about Salima's values? I know for a fact that she forces some of the girls to give private massages for money in the back of the salon. I hear too much whispering to ignore it. So it's like prostitution and I can't have that in my salon. I could be closed down if the police find out it's really happening."

"Have you approached her and asked?" Amina asks.

"She'll only lie," I say. "She lies about everything. Even if it's something insignificant, Salima will lie. She's a habitual liar."

"It sounds like she hasn't gotten over her issues with her husband," Amina says. "Maybe she'll be alright. She probably just needs some time to heal."

"I don't know how much more time I can give her," I respond. "That's why I'm hoping your good nature will rub off on her."

"Well, I'd love to meet her," Amina says. "When do you want to introduce me to her?"

"I was thinking now," I say.

"Oh! Now?" Amina replies. "I have so many things to finish up today. Lisa will kill me if I leave without telling her. She'll know I didn't finish what she wanted me to do."

"Let me worry about Lisa," I say. "Get dressed so we can leave now."

"Kevin, I don't mean to disobey you but you're putting

me in a bad position," Amina protests.

"I told you to let me worry about Lisa," I reply.

"Well…at least let me call her," Amina says. "But wait. I'm not supposed to make calls on the phone." She turns to me. "Can you call her, Kevin, and let her know what's going on?"

"Amina, please!" I say, frustrated. "I told you to let me worry about Lisa. I just need you to get dressed so we can go."

"Can you at least call her while I'm getting dressed?" Amina asks.

I'm not sure why but I see fear and distress in her eyes.

"I'll take care of everything," I say as I pull her up off the couch. "Just go upstairs and get dressed."

"OK, Kevin," Amina says. "I hope you don't get me into trouble."

As Amina goes upstairs, I'm struck by her innocence. She seems such a pure soul.

"Salima definitely needs some of Amina to rub off on her," I say to myself. "I hope my plan to bring them to-gether to be friends works."

Amina

The ride through Harlem and down 125th Street is amaz-ing. It's the first time I've had the chance to feel the pulse of the city.

Alou is foremost in my mind. Every time I see a police

car, I look in the back seat. It's irrational of me to think that I will see him. But I have hope. He may still be here, some-where, looking for me, too.

Kevin is driving the same route as the policemen so we are basically following them. I watch as they make a right turn. Down the street I see ten or more other police cars.

"Kevin, why are there so many police on that street? Is there a problem?" I ask.

"Oh, no. That's the station house for the 25th Precinct," he tells me. I have to remember the street. 119th Street.

It truly is a blessing to be well-protected and to feel safe. America may have its problems, but the safety of its citizens is important. So I can't understand how an African woman who has earned the right to stay in this county would jeop-ardize her life by stealing. Could Kevin be right about Sal-ima? I guess I'm about to find out for myself what's true.

When we get out of the car, Kevin leads the way to a fancy building with sparkling glass windows and a huge awning that holds a sign that reads "125th Hair Braiding Salon."

"Everyone? This is Amina," Kevin announces when we walk through the door. "She's who I've been telling you about."

"Hi, Amina!" they shout at me, just about in unison.

"Hello, everyone," I reply. "It's a pleasure to meet you."

Kevin introduces me to everyone individually. I learn

their names and a little about each of them. Then he invites me to tell them a little about myself.

Kevin saves Salima for last. I see he's extra careful with her, which I assumed he would be considering she's the primary reason I have been brought into the salon.

"Salima, Amina is from West Africa just like you," Kevin says. "But it's hard for me to believe because you two are just so different!"

"If you live here long enough, you'll change, too," Salima tells me. "Don't be foolish like I was and think that life here will be as easy as it was in Africa. Sure, there are many more opportunities here, and that is a blessing. But with some blessings come curses."

"Sometimes you just have to have faith," I say, "and believe wholeheartedly that Allah will pull you through the bad times. I believe that the elders in the tribe didn't speak in vain. They are wise beyond my years. I doubt they'd lead me wrong. Do you think that they'd lead us wrong?"

"I'll come back for you shortly, Amina," Kevin interrupts. He seems satisfied with the direction of the conversation. "So long, ladies."

"Bye, Kevin," they all reply.

I feel the tension in the air subside and realize the workers are thankful that he's brought me into the shop to talk to Salima. Yet I feel a huge rush of anxiety sweep through me. I hope Kevin isn't gone long. I have a long list of chores to finish and I'm afraid Lisa and I will get into it later.

"Amina! Are you listening to me?" Salima asks.

"I'm sorry," I say when I let go of my thoughts. "What were you saying?"

"I asked if you thought the elders would be here to protect you?" Salima asks.

"Allah will always protect me if I live in the right way," I reply. "If we live with the right values and follow the lessons of the elders then Allah will never have a reason to frown upon us."

"You're more naïve than I thought," Salima says.

"Naïve?" I ask. "Why does being grounded in tradition and values make me naïve?"

"Because you're living in a dog-eat-dog world here and you're trying to pretend that's not how it is," Salima says. "But that *is* how it is. You have to learn to adapt to your environment. The ways of the elders in Africa were good for our villages and good for our land. But since that is no longer our land, we cannot live the same way. We'd be eaten alive here if we are naïve. I have the bruises to prove my point."

"Allah heals all of our bruises," I say. "The fact that Allah heals us proves my point. But that brings up a good question. You have healed on the outside, but have you allowed yourself to heal on the inside?"

A look comes over Salima's face that tells me I may just be getting to her.

"Girl, I'm not going to sit here and let you psychoanalyze me," Salima says. "Let's talk about something else.

How do you like America so far?"

"America is a beautiful place though I admit I haven't seen much," I say. "My life here has been complicated so far."

"I know," Salima says. "Kevin told us about what happened to your fiancé. When INS gets involved, it's serious. You need to try to get him out of your head and move on with your life."

"That's easier said than done especially when I don't know for sure what happened to him," I say. "But I have to admit that Lisa keeps me very busy."

"Oh, Lisa," Salima says, rolling her eyes. "How's that situation working out for you?"

"It's horrible," I reply honestly. "She's always on my case. I can't seem to do anything right. From where I'm standing, Lisa doesn't do anything but boss me around. She's very critical of me."

"Lisa is a lazy bitch," Salima states. "I know she doesn't do shit because she *never* did shit. If you cook once a week or clean the house once a month, that's more than Lisa ever did. It's a shame, too. She has a responsibility to his daughter as well."

"You know, the first time I cleaned, it seemed to me that things were much dirtier than they should have been if someone had been cleaning regularly," I say. "But now it's easier to maintain the house."

"Wait! She has you cleaning?" Salima asks.

"And cooking. Every day," I reply.

59

"What does Lisa do?" Salima asks.

"She described her role as my supervisor," I say while glancing at the clock. "Is that the time? Oh! I hope Kevin hurries back. I don't want Lisa to hassle me. If I don't finish the list of things she left for me to do…"

"Wow. She has you shook," Salima says. "Where does she go while you're slaving?"

"I have no idea," I reply. "All I know is that I appreciate the peace and quiet when she's gone. But what do you mean by the term shook?"

"Scared, nervous, timid, petrified…afraid," Salima says.

"I'm definitely not afraid of Lisa," I say. "But I am afraid of being homeless. What if she makes Kevin put me out on the street? She dangles that threat in front of me all day, every day. I do what I have to because I don't have a choice. I'm in a perilous situation. And until I can find Alou…"

"I remember when I had to put her in her place and let her know that she couldn't run shit here," Salima interrupts. "She tried to get Kevin to fire me. When he wouldn't, she stopped coming around. Now she can't stand this place. She probably can't stand me either, but I don't give a fuck."

"Why does everyone talk like that around here?" I ask. "You would never hear that type of language in my village."

"Girl, you need to loosen up," Salima says. "You are wound too tightly. At some point, you're going to realize that it ain't where you're from it's where you're at."

"You're crazy," I say with a smile. I do feel myself loosening up with Salima, however. "You know, Salima, I have an idea."

"Oh lord, I'd better brace myself," she says, jokingly.

"I like you," I say. "And I'm not just saying that. I really like you. I was thinking if I could move in with you, then I wouldn't have to deal with Lisa anymore. Of course I would still take care of Aaliyah. She's a sweetheart and I love her. But dealing with Lisa every day is tearing me apart."

"Oh...wow. Move in with me?" Salima asks. "That right there...that's kind of complicated."

"Why?" I ask. "I like you and hope you like me. We're from the same place so we understand each other. And the things I don't understand, maybe you could school me on and help me. I think it would be good for both of us."

"This is really awkward, Amina," Salima says. "I'm not one to hold my tongue normally, but I did just meet you. And you are from the Motherland. You'll be dumbfounded by things people take for granted here."

"That was mean, Salima," I say. "I don't get dumbfounded by much. I'm a very quick learner."

Not liking where Amina is taking the conversation, Salima decides to just spit out what she's been holding back.

"Amina, you can't move in with me because I have a girlfriend living with me," Salima says.

"Is that all?" I ask. "You already have a friend staying with you and you're worried she won't like me? We can all be friends! I don't need my own room. I can sleep on your couch. That's where I stay now. But at least I won't have to deal with Lisa's constant scrutiny."

"Amina, if you were a light bulb you'd barely be ten watts," Salima says. "You don't understand. I have a *girl-friend*. She won't let you move in with me. Things would not be happy happy, joy joy between the three of us. My girl is too jealous and possessive. I can see her pitching a fit right now."

"I guess I am missing something," I say. "It's not like I'm trying to steal her away from you. OK, she's your friend. I could be your friend as well. Like I said, we can all be friends."

Salima seems exasperated. "Amina, I am a lesbian. My girlfriend is a lesbian. The two of us are lesbians together. That's why we live together. Haven't you ever heard of the saying, 'two's company but three's a crowd?'"

"Lesbian? You can't be a lesbian," I say.

"Why not?" Salima asks.

"Because that's just not acceptable," I reply. "Allah does not accept that from us."

"And who says? The elders?" Salima asks.

"Not only the elders," I reply. "It is in the Koran. It is also in the Bible."

"Are you about to sit here and judge me?" Salima asks. "You don't even know me. You know nothing about her. You just met me. Minutes ago you were asking to move into my house and now you're judging me."

"It's not up to me to judge you," I say. "*Let he that's*

without sin cast the first stone. I cannot judge you and I'm not judging you. The law of the most high is what it is. It speaks for itself. Whether we are in Africa or America, it does not change. I'm sorry if I offended you but you caught me off guard. It would not have occurred to me that someone who's been grounded in the morals of our tribes would take the path that you have. It's just a big surprise to me."

"You are being very judgmental whether you know it or not," Salima says. "And you're going on and on with it. If you mean to apologize, your apology is becoming tedious. Please, stop worrying about me and my life. You have enough things to worry about with your own life. Stop worrying about me licking pussy and worry about where you're going to be sleeping tonight, tomorrow night, and many nights after that."

I cringe at Salima's words. "You can just say it like that?" I ask. "And you're not embarrassed?"

"Hell no! I'm not embarrassed about who I am and nei-ther is my girlfriend. She has overcome huge obstacles. She…oh never mind. You wouldn't understand," Salima says. "But let me ask you. Are you embarrassed about being an eye blink away from homelessness? How about that? Stop coming at my neck and start worrying about your own predicament."

"What do you mean she has overcome huge obstacles? What did she have to overcome?" I ask.

"Oh, Amina," Salima sighs heavily. "The things you

don't know about life would fill a room." She hesitates a second, seeming to weigh whether or not she should tell me her girlfriend's business. "A few years ago, my friend – since you are more comfortable with that term – was married to a man from a neighboring village. Yes, she came here from the Motherland as well. Anyway, her family had made the marriage arrangement the day Lila was born. There was no way for her to get out of it. She would have dishonored her family.

"So she married this man, knowing full well that she did not like men. She had prayed to Allah for help and even discussed her, um, condition with one of the elders. All that did was speed up the wedding. Lila had just turned sixteen.

"Afterwards, she and her husband came here to make a life for themselves. He had family connections so a job was waiting for him. Lila had nothing but his expectations. He wanted to start a family. She could hardly tolerate his touch and made up excuses to avoid his sexual advances. This only bought her a small amount of time. Before long, her husband was beating on her. Her rejection enraged him. And she could not confess what she really was.

"Anyway, one day when he was out at work, Lila snuck out of their house with just the clothes on her back and no one to turn to."

"That is terrible! I'm very sorry, Salima," I say.

"It is terrible. But Allah, as you know, does not forgive homosexuality. The worst part was that my girl...I mean friend, had done nothing wrong. She was being who she was born to be. And not her bastard husband or Allah could change her."

"How did you meet her?" I ask, totally engrossed in the story.

"Lila had nothing but she knew she had to hide. Her husband would have killed her if he found her. For a few days, she lived in one of my neighbor's backyards. I looked out the window early one morning and saw her going through the garbage can. I went down the fire escape and confronted her. She broke down and told me her story," Salima tells me with a sadness in her eyes. "She was so pretty yet so filthy. I took pity on her. I invited her into my home and that is where she has been ever since."

"But you say you are lesbians,"

"Oh, Amina. We truly love each other. Don't you get it? Love is love no matter where it comes from."

"I'm sorry, Salima. I never had to think about things like this," I confess. "I can understand. I am not judgemental. Really. I am sorry. I apologize."

"Maybe then I shouldn't be mad at you for being naïve. You just don't know any better. You're harmless. You don't realize that you're not in some African village. And you are still young and inexperienced in life. Here, you just can't say whatever pops into your mind. You'll get into trouble. So stop doing it! You'll be a dead ass nigga if you keep it up!"

"Why do black people call each other that?" I ask. "I remember Martin Luther King and Malcolm X went through so many pains to stop blacks from being called names. It's like the movement in this country never happened. Where did all the progress go?"

"Amina, I think I love you," Salima says. "You are so naïve. You are so very naïve."

"If you say so," I say.

"I know so," Salima replies. "You're naïve enough to think that life is perfect. It's not. If you live the way the elders tell you to, the way the tribe tells you to, the way the Koran tells you to, the way the Bible tells you to, especially here in Harlem, you can still get busted upside your fucking head and no one will give a shit about you! You need to check some of that shit we learned in Africa at the door. Otherwise, you won't survive here. If I were you, I wouldn't be worried about lesbians or niggas calling each other niggas. I would start worrying about doing whatever it is you have to do to make Kevin and his daughter happy so your black ass isn't thrown out the door! That's where your focus should be right now.

"And if I was Lisa, I'd be mad at you, too. Just look at you with that banging ass and those coconuts up front! You don't even know yet that here in America women wear bras! But I say fuck Lisa! Kevin loves his African bitches and he's especially hot for you, if you haven't noticed."

"You sure are on a roll," I say. "I haven't yet accepted that black people call each other niggas. Now you're telling me that women call each other bitches? What kind of a place is this?"

"This is the type of place where everybody's eating. I

want to eat and if your ass wants to eat, too, you listen to what I'm telling you. Focus on Kevin and his daughter. Fuck Lisa. You already dress half naked around the house so keep acting like you don't know it's inappropriate. Turning Kevin on is a good thing," Salima tells me.

"I'm not trying to entice him in any way," I say. "That's why I don't understand why Lisa feels threatened."

"Amina, you have a lot to learn," Salima says.

"And that's why we should be friends," I say. "You can fill me in on how to survive in America and I can remind you of our traditions."

"I don't need to be preached to," Salima says.

"Baby steps," I reply. "I'm not trying to change you. But from time to time — just in case you want to take baby steps back in the direction from where you came — I may say a thing or two to remind you."

Salima looks at me, a contorted expression on her face.

"I said *baby steps*, Salima," I say.

"OK. But while I'm taking those baby steps, you need to take giant steps in the direction I just told you to go," Salima says. "Your nice ass could save your nice ass when it comes right down to it. American men want nothing more than a nice piece of ass. And Kevin? There's nothing more that he wants than a nice piece of *African* ass. I've seen how he behaves around here. You are good looking — better looking even — than most of the girls that come through here. Amina, you have to use what you've got to get what you want. If you don't want to be homeless, you'd better start paying attention to the fact that Kevin can't stop himself from paying attention to you. If I was you, I'd turn up the heat in subtle ways. Rub your ass against him when you're in tight spots. Wear a see-through nightshirt to bed and walk him to the door wearing it in the morning. You know Lisa's lazy ass will still be in bed that early in the morning so don't worry about her. As long as you keep cleaning the place and cooking for Aaliyah, Lisa will be happy. So stop worrying about morals and start worrying about saving your pretty ass."

"I hear you but what about Alou?" I ask. "I have to find out what happened to him. I can't just accept this life without trying!"

"I don't know what I can do for you there," Salima replies. "But I'll try to help you. I know many people from back home. I'll start asking around. Maybe someone has heard what happened to him."

I am so relieved that she will help me. "Salima, thank you so much. You have helped me a great deal today. I hope in some small way, I have helped you, too."

"You know, I was just thinking that you're not all that bad, girlfriend!"

****

I look out the salon's window for the tenth time and still no sign of Kevin. In the middle of the day, traffic is light and I would recognize his car if I saw it. But I don't and I'm getting frustrated.

Another police car rolls by. After the story Salima told me, I feel safer knowing that the police patrol the streets.

What the...? All of a sudden, a black SUV pulls away from the curb, tires squealing. Somebody is always in a hurry here. And I'm learning that Harlem can be a dangerous place — especially for pedestrians. That's one lesson Salima doesn't need to teach me.

CHAPTER EIGHT

Peace and Love

Kevin

Amina and Salima are huddled together deep in conversation when I return to the salon. Looks like I've gotten my wish.

"So. Can I depend on Salima doing a better job for me?" I ask when Amina and I are alone in the car.

"Don't be so fast, Kevin," she says. "Fixing Salima is not going to be quick. It's going to be a process. But I think we will be good friends."

"Oh," I say with disappointment. "Well, at least you got the ball rolling. As long as things start to move in the right direction, I'll be happy."

"Speaking of right directions…," Amina says, "Where are we going? I don't remember any of these places."

"You're paying attention," I say, impressed.

"Really, Kevin. Where are we going? I still have so much to do…," Amina protests.

"Calm down," I interrupt. "I'm taking you to a very special place. I guarantee you're going to love it."

"Kevin, I've been gone for hours! And I am so far behind in my chores," Amina whines. "Couldn't we do this some other time?"

"Relax, Amina," I say. "There's no time like the present." But she doesn't so I try to calm her. "I hope you're not thinking about Lisa again. I told you to let me worry about her."

"I just hate not finishing my chores," Amina says.

"Will you stop worrying already?" I say. "If I haven't said it enough I'll say it again. You've been doing a fine job. I have no complaints."

"That's you," Amina says. "Lisa complains all the time."

"I don't know why," I say. "You've accomplished more in a few days than she does in a month. I think it's funny how since you've come here, Lisa wants everything to be immaculate."

"I don't know what I'm supposed to say to that," Amina says.

"Don't say anything," I reply. "Just sit back and enjoy the ride. Allow your mind to ponder the wonderful surprise I have in store for you."

Amina

And I am surprised. Beyond surprised. Kevin has taken me to an African market. With so many people from the Motherland gathered in one place, it almost feels like I'm back in West Africa.

"I never would have imagined that a place like this exists in New York City!" I say in amazement.

"There are many more, too, Amina," Kevin says. "And I plan to show you all of them."

My mind drifts to what Salima told me. Perhaps she is right about Kevin.

"Kevin, before you show me anything else, please allow me to thank you." I lean into him to experiment. I give him a friendly hug and a quick kiss on the cheek.

"How often do you shop here?" I ask as I gauge Kevin's reaction to my touch. It appears he is very pleased with himself for making me happy.

"Honestly, not very often. I don't know how to cook!" he says with a chuckle. "But I wanted to show you this place so you could come here to shop."

"Oh! I certainly will! Look at all the spices and fresh fruits and vegetables!" I say with enthusiasm. "I could spend an entire afternoon here. If only…"

"If only what?" Kevin asks.

"I'd like to shop now if only you hadn't kept me out so long. My chores…," I say.

"You're still thinking about Lisa, aren't you?" Kevin

asks.

"Yes, I am," I answer honestly.

Kevin looks frustrated so I try to explain. "You don't understand, Kevin," I say. "Lisa gives me a very hard time. She hates me. She causes me a lot of stress during the course of my day."

"Lisa doesn't hate you," Kevin says.

"She must! You don't know the half of it because you're out working so hard all day. I try to do my best but it's never good enough. I want to do my best. I believe if I do, then she'll have no reason to get on my case. "

"Let's leave then. I don't want to be the cause of any more stress in your life," Kevin says. "We'll stop at Path-mark to pick up a few things for tonight's dinner. I had my mind set on some African food and was hoping you could prepare a dish or two. But it can wait."

"Kevin, I will come back here to shop and pick up everything I need to make an authentic African meal fit for a king," I promise

Kevin perks up. "You promise?" he asks.

"I just did," I reply.

"Oh, yeah, you just did," Kevin says, embarrassed.

CHAPTER NINE

Friday Drama

Amina

I tuck the money Kevin has given me to go shopping under a couch cushion so Lisa won't find it – though I doubt she'd look. She never bothers with my 'bed'.

While I'm thinking about the menu, I throw a t-shirt over the sheer shirt I slept in last night. Lisa will never see the nightie I wore when I walked Kevin to the door this morning. No way!

I will be smarter and fight harder, just like Salima said, I think to myself as I lay my head back down to get a little bit more rest.

****

I move like a flash after returning from taking Aaliyah to school. Lisa never says a word when she comes downstairs before going to wherever she goes every day, but today I can see in her expression that she's impressed.

I play up the fact that I'm doing this all for her just to keep her off balance. I've begun to realize that she is not really the one in control, as she's led me to believe. I feel myself growing more confident.

Yet I won't allow myself to get cocky. In her presence, I will continue to be the demure, frightened person she thinks I am.

As soon as she walks out the door, however, all those thoughts leave my head. I rush into action to accomplish all that I've planned.

"Please, Kevin, I promise I'm not slacking off," I said earlier. "I really have to pick up some special cleaning supplies to do a few jobs that have been neglected around here. If just for today you could pick Aaliyah up after school, I would appreciate it so much. I would feel terrible if I was just one minute late getting to her school. The stress on me would be too much."

I hated not being honest with Kevin but I needed him to pick up his daughter today. How else would I be able to surprise them?

Kevin

I feel a little tense as I'm waiting for Aaliyah. Once again, Salima is short on the receipts.

"What is taking so long? I thought Amina was making progress with her," I whisper under my breath.

I'm always happy to see my little girl but today I'm confused when I see her skipping toward the car. She's wearing her best Sunday outfit.

"Hi Daddy," Aaliyah says happily as she gets into the car.

"Hi, baby," I reply. "Did you have your picture taken today or something?"

"No, Daddy, we didn't have pictures today," Aaliyah says. "Amina said…"

"Miss," I say, interrupting Aaliyah before she can go on.

"Miss Amina said that she wanted to dress me up special cuz I'm special and today is special," Amina says, beaming.

"She's right, you are special," I reply. Yet, in the back of my mind, I wonder what's going on. *Why would Amina dress my daughter up for no reason?*

Lisa is always a bitch, Salima is robbing me blind, and the last thing in the world I need is for Amina to start tripping on me too.

****

My fears about Amina magnify as we get out of the car. It's entirely too early for Amina to be sleeping yet the house is strangely dark and quiet.

Correction. I see a faint glimmer of light, like maybe the television is on.

Why would the lights be off when she knows we're coming home and haven't eaten dinner yet? I ask myself as I stick my key in the door.

As soon as I open it, my questions are answered.

Right away I feel really guilty and silly. Amina has made a beautiful scene for us. The light I saw from outside turns out to be dozens of little candles that smell like African spices. Or not. When I turn the corner into the dining room, I see the table is perfectly set and steaming plates of authentic African food are spread across it.

"Come in your highness and my princess," Amina says with a curtsy. "Have a seat."

I'm stunned by what she has done for us, and I can't help but notice her African ceremonial garb.

So this is why she had Aaliyah dress up. She planned this exquisite dinner and wanted Aaliyah to feel extra special.

"Amina, you didn't have to do all this!" I exclaim.

"Nonsense!" Amina replies. "You deserve this. You took me in when I had no one. You deserve all this, dear," she says as she turns to Aaliyah. "You look so beautiful!"

"Thank you for dressing me this morning, Miss Amina," Aaliyah says.

"Oh, you're welcome, sweetie," Amina replies. "Now, see this bowl of water and these towels? In Africa, we wash our hands before a feast celebrating an important event. I want you two to know how we do things."

"What's so important, Miss Amina?" Aaliyah asks.

"Well, honey, we are all together and everyone is

happy," Amina says. "You should always show the people you care about that you love them. My way is to cook you a nice meal."

Amina starts tearing up.

I grab her hand and rub it.

"Oh, don't cry. Please," I say.

"I'm just being silly," Amina says. "After you wash your hands, could you lead us in a prayer, Kevin? Then we can eat."

Aaliyah and I dip our fingers into the bowl of warm water and Amina is ready our towels. "Oh no!" she says.

"What is it, Amina?"

"We have to wait! Where is Lisa? What time will she get here? I don't want her to miss out. This is for all of you," she says as she waves her hand across the table.

What an authentic, beautiful girl Amina is. She really means it when she says she appreciates us.

Amina

OK. I lied. Sue me for not being perfect. But remember that no one is perfect.

I wasn't thinking about Lisa when I decided to prepare this feast but now I honestly feel that she should be a part of it — if for no other reason than to get her to eat something other than unhealthy fast food. But maybe it's best she's not here. She has a way of putting a damper on everything.

"Amina? Did you hear me?" Kevin asks.

"Oh, I'm sorry," I say. "I was lost in my thoughts for a moment. What were you saying?"

"I said who knows where Lisa is," Kevin replies. "She prances in whenever she damned well pleases. I don't want to ruin this night. Everything is perfect just the way it is. Let's just start without her. If she shows up, she can heat something up."

"Alright then," I say. "Let's dig in."

I've prepared African vegetables, steamed fish, rice, gravy, corn fritters, and a sampling of African desserts. We cook these things in many African villages at times of great joy. And just like back home, the mood in Kevin's home is happy and joyful.

Kevin is smiling, Aaliyah is beaming, and I'm just soaking it all in. It does my heart good to know that I've made these two people happy. We are all content.

That is until Lisa opens the door. Immediately, the tension in the room is thick enough to cut with a knife.

"Hey, babe! I'm home!" Lisa calls out. "Sorry I'm late but I brought dinner. Why's it so dark in here? What the...?"

She flips on the lights when she turns the corner into the dining room. "What's all this, *Kevin?*" Lisa asks, a nasty edge to her voice. "Amina, what *is* all this?"

Both Kevin and I are silent so it's Aaliyah who blurts out a response. Her childish innocence makes the situation worse.

"Miss Amina made us this big dinner tonight!" Aaliyah exclaims. "And she dressed me up all pretty and everything."

"I thought Friday night dinners were my responsibility," Lisa says. "Amina, didn't we talk about that?"

"I'm sorry, I forgot what day it was," I say.

This time I'm not lying. I really did forget.

"You forgot?" Lisa snaps. "What the hell do you mean you forgot?"

"Lisa, chill," Kevin says. "I'm glad Amina cooked because you're late as usual. My daughter would have been starving."

"Don't do that, Kevin," Lisa says. "I have her favorite right here. Aaliyah, don't you want the Happy Meal I brought you?"

"Lisa, stop it," Kevin says. "Aaliyah is fine. We're all fine. And Amina was thoughtful enough to make enough for all of us. She even asked about you before we started eating. If I didn't put my foot down, we would have still been waiting for you and all this food would have gone cold."

"This is some bullshit!" Lisa says.

"I told you not to curse in front of Aaliyah," Kevin says calmly.

"Oh, I ain't even started, baby," Lisa says. "You better believe that!"

Lisa lunges at the table and starts knocking plates on the

floor.

"I'm not having this bitch keep trying to take you away from me!" Lisa says. "She knows damned well that I take care of dinner on Fridays. And I don't want you and my daughter eating this fucking jungle food!"

"Lisa, stop it!" Kevin says and jumps up to restrain her. "Why are you acting this way?"

"So, you're going to take her side over mine?" Lisa asks. "After all I've done for you, you're going to do me like this?"

"Like what, Lisa?" Kevin asks. "How am I doing you?"

"You're not standing up for me, for one thing," Lisa says. "You're supposed to ride or die with me regardless of — whatever. Now you got this bitch cooking for you. You got her getting all chummy with Aaliyah."

"Aaliyah likes Amina because she spends time with her," Kevin says. "And she's nice to her. How do you expect Aaliyah to feel when you're acting like this? Look at her. You've made her cry."

"Oh, so now you're going to blame that shit on me?" Lisa shouts. "I'll tell you what. Ain't a motherfucking soul gonna eat none of this damned jungle food tonight. That's for damned sure."

Lisa breaks away from Kevin and continues knocking plates onto the floor. Kevin tries his best to grab Lisa and hold her down but she's behaving like a madwoman.

During the turmoil, Aaliyah starts screaming and runs up the stairs. I follow to make sure that she's okay.

We may as well have stayed downstairs because both Kevin and Lisa are screaming so loudly it's like they are in Aaliyah's bedroom with us. I try to cover her young ears and calm her down.

"You are fucking cuckoo," Kevin says.

"Oh, so now you're going to talk shit about me?" Lisa says.

"Everything was going fine until you showed up, late as hell as usual, and turned a nice evening into a terrible one," Kevin says.

"So you're blaming me for everything?" Lisa asks.

"Who else threw the damned food on the floor?" Kevin asks.

"It's fucking jungle food!" Lisa screams.

"What are you talking about? It's better than anything you've ever served us," Kevin says.

"Now you're criticizing my cooking, too?" Lisa asks. "That's why I don't do shit for your ass!"

"You've never done shit for me!" Kevin hollers.

"See...there you go again," Lisa says. "Everything was fine until this African bitch came around here."

"This doesn't have shit to do with Amina," Kevin says. "This is about you. This is about you not putting a thing into this relationship and about all the shit you've been taking out. It's not fair and it's not right. I give you everything. What the hell do you give me in return?"

"Now you're complaining about everything!" Lisa screams. "I already told that bitch she's gonna be a problem."

"Look at you. You're blaming shit on someone else," Kevin says. "You need to fix you."

"Oh, so I'm not good enough for you?" Lisa asks.

Kevin doesn't answer or at least he doesn't answer fast enough to satisfy Lisa.

"Well, fuck you then!" Lisa shouts. "I hope you and your African bitch are happy together. I'm leaving and I'm never coming back. I hope you shit out your intestines fucking with that damned jungle food!"

Next thing I hear is the door slamming.

I remain with Aaliyah on her little bed, trying to comfort her and wondering what is going to happen next.

CHAPTER TEN

Breaking Up

Lisa

I'm so livid, I'm shaking. I jump in my SUV and pop Li'l Kim's Naked Truth into my CD player, pushing the volume up, hoping it'll drown out my thoughts. I'm driving to I don't know where, trying to navigate my swirling thoughts instead of the damned streets.

After a while, I realize I've ended up close to Michelle's house so I decide to visit my sister and fill her in on what's been happening. I'm hoping that her opinionated ass is able to remember that blood is thicker than water when she starts dishing out her opinions about who's right and who's wrong.

I park the car and take the stairs two at a time. My legs are screaming at me because I haven't been to the gym in what seems like a eternity but I know I'll look better than my sister.

I ring the bell and it takes her forever to get to the door. She flips on the outside light. Then it takes her for forever to let me in.

Michelle's wearing her old-lady housecoat that she says is comfortable but looks like shit. "Lisa, what are you doing here?" Michelle asks. "You know I don't open my door after dark. How come you didn't at least call me before you came?"

"I keep trying to tell you that everything doesn't just fall neatly into place, Michelle," I reply sarcastically as I push past Michelle's irritated face. "When you're living life, you have to take it as it comes. Sometimes it's not as peachy for everybody else like it is for you out here in fairy tale land."

"Excuse you! You're the one showing up at my house in the middle of the damned night!" Michelle says as she locks the door after me. "You should have left that attitude with whoever upset you. Don't be bringing it to me like I did something to you. Now, what's wrong?"

"You're right. I apologize," I reply. The last thing I need is for Michelle to kick me out on my ass. And she would do it, too, before I even got out one word of explanation. So even though I don't feel sincere when I apologize, I do it. Maybe she'll even find an inconsequential amount of compassion for her little sister.

"That African bitch is trying to break up my relationship," I snap.

"Lisa…your language," Michelle says quickly.

"Sweetie, now is not the time for rules," I reply. "I'm over here and that African bush bitch is at my house with my man."

"Lisa, you know my kids are here," Michelle says. "They're in bed but they aren't asleep yet. You know we don't curse around our children."

Again, I feel like I need to fall back since I don't want to be put out by Miss Prissy. I try to calm down enough to communicate with her in the fake, phony way that she — and all of her religious friends — do.

"OK, let me figure out where to start," I say and take a deep breath. "I told that wench not to do anything without asking my permission. If she had asked me about dressing Aaliyah up and cooking a big, special dinner on my night to cook, I would have told her no. She should have known it was absolutely out of the question."

"So you're mad because she cooked dinner tonight?" Michelle asks. "I thought you make her cook and clean the house because, as you put it, room and board are not free."

"Hold up," I say defensively. "That's part of it but it's not all of it. She's never supposed to cook on Friday nights. That's the night I bring Aaliyah her favorite Happy Meal from McDonalds."

"McDonalds, Lisa?" Michelle asks. "Come on."

"Now you know that Mom ain't never cooked on no-body's Friday," I reply.

"You're right about that," Michelle agrees. "Come to think of it, Mom never cooked on Saturday either."

"That's what I'm saying," I say excitedly. I'm relieved that my sister is finally seeing eye to eye with me. "The way that wench is cooking and cleaning, all I know is she's trying to turn Kevin against me. And I can't believe he wouldn't stop eating when I told him to. I'm disappointed in him for not having my back."

"I do agree that most working mothers don't cook on Friday nights, maybe not even Saturday night. But as a parent, if I had the choice between having my child eat a balanced home cooked meal or fast food, I'm with Kevin. I'd choose a home cooked meal," Michelle says.

"Not you, too!" I reply in frustration.

"What do you mean, *not me too?*" Michelle asks.

"You're supposed to be on my side!" I say. "Why is everybody in this African bitch's corner? Wait. Don't even say anything. I apologize for cursing. My bad."

"Sweetie, listen," Michelle says as she puts her arm around me. "I love you and I'm going to always be on your side. But part of being on your side is telling you the truth and not just saying what you want to hear. That would be fake or phony like you always say I am. But I'm not at all *fake.*"

I almost chuckle at the way Michelle stresses the word fake.

"I said that most mothers who work hard all week don't cook on Fridays," Michelle continues. "But keep it real with yourself, Lisa. You don't do anything. Kevin is taking care of you. The least you can do for your big Friday nights is to have a nice home cooked meal waiting for him."

"But I just told you that Aaliyah and I have this ritual," I reply defensively.

"I know, I know. Happy Meals," Michelle says. "But have you ever asked her what foods she really likes."

I start laughing and say, "That girl loves rice and gravy. If she could eat that for breakfast, lunch and dinner, she would."

"OK. So why not make her rice and gravy with the right meat on a Friday?" Michelle asks. "Before you told them to stop eating, did you notice if rice and gravy was included in the meal the girl prepared?"

"As a matter of fact, they were," I reply. "But what difference does that make? It was still my night!"

"Lisa, you'd better wake up and smell the coffee," Michelle says. "This woman is trying to connect with Kevin's daughter on one level. She's trying to connect with him on another. OK, so you're in charge. We both know how much you like to run the show. But at the end of the day, you have to fight fire with fire. You can't be the school disciplinarian when you have another person in there spoiling your man and his child rotten. Momma used to always say that you get more with honey than with vinegar. You need to soften up and get with the program. My man doesn't run me either but I know enough to make him feel loved. That's why he's given me these wonderful children, this nice house and a new car every three years. I'm not tooting my own horn but sometimes you have to play the game the way it needs to be played, not just how you want to play it. Relationships are give and take. When this other girl is cleaning the house, cooking the meals, doing the laundry, taking Aaliyah to and from school, what are you doing that Kevin can point out is helping the relationship? When was the last time you helped his daughter with her homework? Haven't you heard that the hand that rocks the cradle rules the world?"

Michelle's starting to make a little bit of sense to me. But she's still missing my point. My man is supposed to have my back. Period!

"What's the matter? Cat got your tongue?" Michelle asks.

"I don't know," I reply. "This is all so confusing. Everything happened so fast. I didn't see any of this coming."

"And that was your first mistake," Michelle says. "Maybe you didn't have much say about letting her come into the house. But you should not have let her have as much leeway as you have."

"But I never give her leeway," I respond. "I've been on her like white on rice. I barely let her breathe."

"That's how you are when you're there, Lisa. But how often are you there?" Michelle asks. "Where were you when she was cooking this big, extravagant meal? If you don't want her spending so much time with Aaliyah, then you spend the time with Aaliyah and learn all her favorite foods and things to do. This girl didn't figure all these things out on her own."

"You're right, I should be there more often," I say.

"Hello? Some African chick moves in the house and I'm not going to be there twenty-four seven?" Michelle asks. "And he already has a salon filled with African women? He must have a thing for them. You remember how much stuff you dealt with before over his African manager?"

"Yeah but Kevin doesn't like her like that," I reply. "She's married."

"She's not too married if her husband is locked up at Sing Sing," Michelle says. "But I'm not saying that his manager is the problem. His fascination with African women, though, may be a problem. That's why you have to step your game up."

"Step my game up?" I ask.

"Yes! Step your game up," Michelle says. "Mop his floors, wash his dirty drawers, cook his meals, sex him up. Whatever it takes."

"That's another thing," I say. "He used to beg me for it all the time. Now that this ho's moved in, we don't have sex anymore."

"You said that she just turned seventeen so I don't think Kevin would have sex with her," Michelle says, "but don't put it past him. You don't know if she's throwing herself on him or not. If I were you, I'd keep my eyes open with Miss Amina. But, and this is a big but, you can't put it all on her. Anything you don't want her doing for Kevin and Aaliyah, do yourself. You have to let him see that he doesn't need her to take care of him and his daughter. You're all the woman he needs. Then, once you have firmly convinced him, start making demands. Your first demand should be a timetable for Miss Amina to get her butt out of the house and live somewhere else. But while this process is going on, and it's going to take time, you can't be acting violent or jealous. That will push Kevin away and you'll end up losing him for good."

"So knocking all the food she cooked off the table in a rage is not what I was supposed to do?" I ask.

"I knew you did something crazy like that," Michelle says, laughing.

"I was pissed," I admit. "What was I supposed to do?"

"Well, it's not like you can take it back now," Michelle says. "It already happened. The good thing is that if Kevin loves you, he's not going to just be done with you over this one incident. You have time to turn things around. If I was you, I would go back to him and make nice. Then sex him up so bad that he can't even walk. You should like that since you're such a freak."

"Hey, don't hate the player. Hate the game," I say, feeling myself perk up.

"You'd just better get better at playing the game," Michelle says. "But seriously, I love you. I know that there's another woman in your house and that's wrong. Yet I don't think that Kevin is sleeping with her. So don't do anything stupid and get yourself in trouble."

"Me? Moi?" I ask innocently.

"I'm serious, Lisa," Michelle says. "We all have our moments, but I do love you very much. Knowing that you're OK means a lot to me. My kids would die if something happened to their crazy auntie. Sometimes I think we all live vicariously through you. Just think before you act. Don't put the blame on everyone else. If you step your game up, you won't have anything to worry about. I may not agree with everything you do or the way you dress or the fact that you don't go to church as often as you're supposed to…"

"Is there a point to this?" I interrupt.

"The point is, Lisa, if you come at a man the way you're supposed to come at him, I don't think that there's another woman who can compete with you," Michelle says. "Look at you. You're beautiful. And you're sexy to boot."

"Aw, that's so sweet," I say.

"But don't think your good looks are going to get you by this time like they used to," Michelle warns. "Put in some work. Put in the work and I promise you that you'll get good results."

"Thanks, sis, for being here for me," I say. "I needed to have this discussion with you. And it helped. It really helped."

"Actions speak louder than words, Lisa," Michelle says. "Don't let that fiery temper of yours get the better of you."

"I know, I know… don't do anything else stupid," I say.

"You'd better not," Michelle replies. "If they lock your butt up, I'm coming to jail to kick it."

"Listen to you!" I say, laughing. "Now that's the girl I remember growing up with!"

"That girl died a long time ago," Michelle says. "But I will bring her back from time to time if I have to. I didn't like the way your spirit looked when you first walked in. I have to do what I have to do to protect you."

"Aw, I love you big sis," I say.

"I love you too, Lisa," Michelle says. "I mean it. I love you."

We hug, say our goodbyes, and I'm on my way, wondering if I'll heed any of the sound advice my big sister gave me.

CHAPTER ELEVEN

Back to the Salon

Lisa

I sneak back into the house, close the door lightly, and tip-toe over to Amina so as to not wake her.

I stand over her quietly for a second, salivating at the thought of slitting her throat right.

After staring at her so long, she starts to disgust me. I place my scarf over her nose and mouth and whisper in her ear as she is startled awake. I don't want her to scream and wake up Aaliyah or Kevin.

"You may think you won round one, you fake-ass, African, slut-ho," I whisper vehemently. "But you've got another thing coming. I'm the big fish in this pond and you ain't got shit on me. You're just a scared-ass little girl and I'm a grown-ass woman. Yeah, you may be cute. You may have a nice little shape. But my shape is full grown. You can't compete with me. You're an amateur. You're in the little league and I'm a professional. I want you to listen to my man moan when I go upstairs and put it on him. I own his mind. I own his thoughts. But don't get it fucked up. Although, I know you can't fuck with me, that doesn't mean you won't get yourself hurt if you keep trying to. Play with me one more time and try to turn my man and his daughter against me and it's gonna be a problem."

I twist the skin on Amina's arm for good measure to emphasize what I'm saying.

"You've run out of strikes. When I say we're going to see if you can get it right tomorrow, and the day after that, and the day after that, I'm not fucking around with you. Play with me if you want and I'll show you that there will be consequences and repercussions for taking my kindness for weakness. I'm done playing games with you. I'm about to start showing you that I mean what the fuck I say."

* * * *

After setting Amina straight, I go upstairs to deal with Kevin. Yeah, I'm mad as hell at him but Michelle is right. Sometimes you have to fight fire with fire. One thing that Amina can't compete is that I'm fucking Kevin and she isn't. But even if she was, I know my shot is better than hers. At any rate, I don't want to give Kevin any reason to want to find out.

After I close our bedroom door, I tiptoe over to Kevin, take my clothes off, and slip into bed beside him.

I start rubbing on his more than adequate manhood until I wake up both heads.

"Shhhhh," I say while placing my finger over his mouth. "Don't say anything. Just accept my apologies and let me take care of you the way you like me to."

Without saying another word my head disappears under the sheets. I perform surgery on him until I have him squealing. Then I ease up with my mouth because I'm not ready for him to release just yet.

I pull myself back up to eye level with him and straddle my man the way he likes me to. Then I start riding him like Lisa Bonet rode Mickey Rourke in Angel Heart.

My fuck game is serious and judging by the way he's calling my name and moaning up a storm, Amina is getting an earful downstairs of just how serious my lovemaking with Kevin is.

It doesn't matter what else she's thinking. At the end of the day, I'm sure she'll understand what I said. She's a little girl trying to compete in a grown woman's game. She may as well fold her hand because there's no way she can win.

Amina

I'm not physically attracted to Kevin so Lisa having sex with him doesn't bother me the way she thinks it will and wants. Alou is still primary in my mind.

I quickly get bored with them having sex and fall back

to sleep. Before you know it, my alarm is ringing. It's time to make a quick meal for Aaliyah and get her ready for school.

****

I peep in on Lisa before I leave. I'm careful not to open or close the door too quickly, but I do want to get a look at her to figure out how much time I think I have. She's butt naked in the bed and out like a light.

She's as lazy as Salima says she is, I think to myself with a chuckle. *But Lisa isn't lying. She does have a really nice body. I wish my boobs were as big as hers.*

I stop comparing my body to hers when I hear Aaliyah call for me from downstairs. The last thing I want is to be in Lisa's room when she wakes up.

I tiptoe out of the room and softly close the door.

"Coming, sweetie!" I say as I make my way back down the stairs.

****

Salima is happy to see me when I visit her at the salon. But I make it clear I'm not there for small talk. I pull her aside and immediately tell her about last night with Lisa.

"Are you serious?" Salima asks. "She knocked all the food on the floor?"

"She sure did," I say. "But what Kevin said after she left made up for it. He said that he'd rather eat my food off the floor than touch any of the McDonald's Lisa bought. Then Aaliyah co-signed it."

"OK. Cosigned," Salima says. "I see you've been paying attention to some of the slang I've been trying to teach you."

"Whatever," I say with a smile.

"You're right, though. It's a very big deal that he and his daughter agreed," Salima says.

"And then Kevin grabbed Aaliyah's hand and they went into the kitchen together and threw her McDonald's away," I say, beaming.

"See? I told you that you have his mind," Salima says. "Now you have to capture his body."

"Speaking of that…Lisa came back after everybody was asleep and threatened me," I tell her. "Then she went upstairs and had sex with Kevin. I don't know what she was doing to him but she was either killing him or brainwashing him. Whatever the case, he was having a better time with her than I could ever give him."

"Don't say that!" Salima says. "You're dead wrong. You don't think Kevin doesn't fantasize about being with you? It's not until a man has been with a woman a few times that he starts making demands and wanting more from her."

"I still don't know why you think he wants me so much," I say.

"That's because you don't know American men like I do," Salima says. "American men are the worst. They just may be the most perverted men in the world."

98

"I thought English men were," I say.

"The English are perverted, too!" Salima says. "But how do you think the United States got started? The first settlers here were degenerates from England. They colonized the U.S. territories. They pretty much stole it from the native American Indians. The Revolutionary War was about getting out from under England's control. You'd better learn American history if you have thoughts about becoming a U.S. citizen."

"I do want to become a citizen," I say, "but not right now. Right now I don't need a history lesson. I need to know how to deal with Lisa."

"Fuck Lisa!" Salima spits. "I told you that already! You need to concentrate on Kevin. So far you're doing everything right. Taking care of him and Aaliyah is the most important thing. Yes, you're cooking and cleaning for them and making sure that they are happy. But for whatever reason, you refuse to throw yourself at him like I tell you to."

"Why does everything have to be about sex?" I ask.

"Amina, you are so damned naïve!" Salima says, completely exasperated. "If I was you, I'd wake up and smell the coffee. You need to realize that you have problems. For one, Alou is gone and not coming back for you."

"How can you be so sure? What if he's out on the streets looking for me,"

"Girl, please! Stop being so foolish!" Salima tells me.

"It has always been my family's dream for one of us to be in America. I don't want to go back," I confess.

"That's better," Salima says. "So how are you going to stay here?"

"Kevin?" I ask dejectedly.

"That's right. Your husband is gone and your tourist visa will expire," Salima says. "What will you do then?"

"I don't know," I admit honestly.

"Exactly. You don't know," Salima says. "Kevin is a good man and he's attracted to you. You don't realize how critical your situation is. You need to start solidifying your position in Kevin's household. You can't depend on the African women here in this salon or any of the others you might meet in the streets. Africans are divided in this country. It's not like it is back home. Everything isn't all good. You might believe that everything is fine between you and another African woman. But if she was in the same boat as you are now in, she'd fuck the shit out of Kevin and try to get him to marry her."

"Is it that bad?" I ask.

"How bad do you think it would be to go back to your village in shame after squandering your family's resources?" Salima asks. "This is a cutthroat society. Everybody doesn't love you here."

"Remind me why I would want to stay here," I tell her.

"Because there really are more opportunities here than there ever could be in Africa," Salima says. "You just have to learn how to deal with the mental aspect of America. Just toughen up a bit. Then you will be able to take things for what they are. You'll appreciate the opportunities if you

stop letting yourself get bogged down with African traditions. Yeah, a strong community is a good thing. But with
everybody dirt poor, how good could it be? Believe me, if
that is how you see your future, you don't want to go
back."

"I hear what you're saying, and I agree that my family
would be disappointed if I was deported," I say, "but I'm
still not sure Alou isn't out there right now looking…"

"Forget Alou!" Salima interrupts. "You need to seduce
Kevin and make him fall in love with you."

"You're talking about sex again?" I ask.

"No, not exactly," Salima says. "You have to make him
think that the opportunity for sex is there. You have to let
him know that you want him in that way. It doesn't matter
how much you tease him, though. You cannot go all the
way with him and give it up before he marries you. Why
would he buy the cow if he's getting the milk for free? Once
he marries you, you can start the process of getting your
U.S. citizenship. You'll live in his house for free, you won't
have to pay any bills, you won't have to worry about rent,
and if you play your cards right, soon you'll be co-owner of
this salon. You have to take my advice, Amina. I'm not trying to steer you wrong."

"You really think Kevin likes me like that?" I ask, a little
uncertain.

"He adores you!" Salima says. "Why can't you see that?
And Aaliyah adores you, too. I was shocked when you told
me that both of them would have rather eaten your home

cooked food off the floor than eat McDonalds. Don't you see that Kevin did not want to hurt your feelings? You're on the right track, Amina. Keep doing what you're doing. Now all you have to do is turn up the heat and make him believe that something physical is going to pop off between the two of you in the near future."

"You make it sound so easy," I say.

"When it comes to a man wanting a piece of ass it doesn't get any easier," Salima says. "All you have to do is shake your ass, add water and stir. The rest of the recipe is already written. He's a horny-ass man just like the rest of them."

I look at the clock on the wall and realize that I've been gone longer than I wanted.

"Well, thanks for the advice. But I have to get back before Lisa wakes up. She's such a bitch! I don't want to make things worse."

"You don't have to tell me, girl," Salima says. "You do not have to tell me!"

CHAPTER TWELVE

Hate

Amina

I hail a taxi at the corner and on the ride home, I think about what Salima said. It bothers me that she is so positive that Alou is gone for good. It bothers me that she doesn't understand why I hesitate with Kevin.

I start dusting as soon as I get in. Five minutes later, I hear Lisa get out of bed. She would have flipped out if I was not already cleaning when she woke up. I'm glad I can justify the extra expense of taking a taxi.

"Make sure you do a damn good job!" Lisa says when she comes down the stairs.

Her ignorance and bad manners don't surprise me. She never says good morning to me. She never speaks to me when she gets home, either.

"Once I get myself together we're gonna sit down and have a little talk," Lisa says snidely. "You've been showing

your ass around here lately, going way outside of my comfort zone, and we're gonna get this shit under control."

I dread the thought of sitting down and talking to Lisa.
She's the worst type of human being imaginable. I don't
want any part of her evilness and shadiness to rub off on
me. I want to remain decent.

After she leaves the kitchen, now that I know that she's
awake, I feel like it's OK for me to wash the breakfast
dishes. I washed the dishes once before Lisa got out of bed
and she acted like she was about to have a coronary.

"Bitch, I know you're just trying to be smart!" she
screamed down the stairs. "You'd better not make me come
the fuck downstairs and show you what damned time it is!"

I thought she would be happy. I was cooking for her
and cleaning up after her. At the very least, I was helping
her keep the peace. Kevin and Lisa hadn't argued lately
about her not keeping the house the way he wanted.

But later for Lisa. I can't take her too seriously. I'll just
do what needs to be done until I figure out what else I am
going to do.

"Alright, bitch," Lisa says, bumping her way noisily into
the kitchen. "I need to go over the ground rules again because I think you're starting to believe that your shit don't
stink. I have no reason to be nice to you so I won't be. As a
matter fact, I hate your fucking guts. For the last fucking
time, I'm going to tell you to stay the fuck away from my
daughter and definitely stay the hell away from my man. All
you need to do is wake your ass up in the morning, do your

chores, and stay the fuck out of my way. You need to be as inconspicuous as possible. Don't nobody need to be talking about you because nobody needs to be around you long enough to know what's up with you. And, to be clear, by nobody I mean Aaliyah and Kevin. Matter fact, stay the fuck away from me, too. Every time I see you I feel like I'm about to throw up. I gave you the ground rules a long time ago and lately you've been slippin'. You can best believe, though, that this is the last time I plan on talking to you about anything. After this, I guarantee you I'll be bringing you pain."

With that, Lisa turns and leaves the kitchen. I hear the front door open and close and I know she's gone to wherever it is she goes every day. I would love to know what Lisa's up to. But for now, I'm just happy she's gone. I can do my work in peace.

✳✳✳✳

Around two, the phone rings. I know it's Kevin. He calls me every afternoon. I have to admit, he's very thoughtful.

"Hi Kevin! How are you today?"

"I'm fine," Kevin says. "How are things with you?"

"I'm managing," I say. "I've finished cleaning and am waiting for the meat to thaw so I can start dinner."

"You're such a good woman, Amina. One of these days you're going to make a terrific wife," he says.

"If I ever find Alou…," I say wistfully. "So, did you call

just to clown around with me?"

"Actually, I'm bored," Kevin says. "I want to eat lunch out today. Not to be insensitive or anything. I'm sure the lunch you packed for me is slamming. But I really just need a change of scenery. Would you like to join me? I'd like to do something special for you."

"I won't be offended if you go out for lunch," I say. "Don't worry about me at all. I'm fine. How do you Americans say it? Do you."

"You're confused, silly!" Kevin says. "It's not about me not eating your food. I want you to accompany me. I'll pick you up in twenty minutes. Can you be ready?"

"Oh. Kevin, I don't think that's such a good idea," I say. "Lisa would kill both of us if she found out we went to lunch together. I think I'm going to have to pass."

"You don't have a choice," Kevin says. "I'm going to do something nice for you and that's final. Get your butt in gear. It'll be a treat for both of us."

"But…but…" I say but the phone has gone dead. All I hear is dial tone.

Trying to make the best out of a potentially bad situation, I scramble to finish as much as I can. I even do all the prep work for dinner, storing the ingredients in the refrigerator so all I'll need to do later is pop everything in the oven and on the stove top.

****

Kevin takes me to a restaurant on 149th Street called Holy Basil. I order coconut milk soup and a green papaya salad with chicken. It is delicious. Kevin orders a curried dish that smells wonderful.

It's nice being out of the house. And it's nice to spend time with Kevin. He really is a good man. Salima may have a point. I should try to think about him on a different level. Even though my heart resists, it's hard to imagine what my life would be like if he hadn't rescued me.

But none of this really matters at the moment. In the back of my mind, I'm worried about Lisa's warning. I have to get home.

* * * *

"Owwww!!!" I cry. Without warning, Lisa backhands me across the face.

I didn't expect her to come home before dinner much less wait for me behind the front door, ready to pounce.

"You thought I was fucking playing with you, didn't you?" Lisa screams. "I just saw Kevin drop your ass off!"

Lisa reprimands me like I'm a child. Her words don't phase me at all but her hitting me is a serious problem.

I cover up as well as I can to try and protect myself, but she keeps wailing on me. Lisa is very heavy-handed. Or she's holding weights. I just pray she tires herself out soon.

An hour later, I examine myself in the mirror. Lisa's gone but the damage she has done remains. I am bruised all over, especially on my face and arms. I honestly feel much worse than I look.

I'll make up a story for Kevin. He can't know Lisa and I got physical.

CHAPTER THIRTEEN

Hiding the Truth

Amina

"Hey, Amina!" Kevin says cheerfully when he gets home from work. "Lunch sure was great today!"

"Mmm hmm," I say unenthusiastically. "It was nice."

Kevin pauses and turns to me. "What's wrong with you?" he asks.

"Oh, nothing. I'm fine," I reply.

"Bull!" Kevin exclaims. "Fine? You normally have more to say."

"Everything is fine," I say as Kevin moves closer.

"What the...? Let me look at you," he says. "Damn! What happened to you?"

"Nothing really," I lie. "I just slipped and fell."

"Slipped and fell? How? When?" Kevin asks. "You don't look like a person who just slipped and fell. Did you hurt your arm? What about your back?"

"I assure you this is all that happened," I say. "Now please get ready for dinner. Aaliyah is in the small bathroom upstairs getting herself together."

"Fine. I'll get myself together," Kevin says. "But I don't know about this. Was Lisa here today when we got back?"

"Why do you ask?" I reply, trying to remain evasive.

"Just curious," Kevin says.

"She was here for a little while then she left," I reply.

"Did she say anything?" Kevin asks.

"Like what?" I ask.

"Just anything?" Kevin asks.

I hunch my shoulders.

"Was she acting funny?" Kevin asks.

"Kevin! Where are you going on with this?" I ask. "I'm sure that Aaliyah is very hungry. Can you please just get yourself cleaned up so that we can feed that darling little girl of yours?"

"Alright...I'll fall back," Kevin says. "But this conversation isn't over. I'm going to get to the bottom of what's going on around here."

Kevin goes upstairs and returns with Aaliyah a few minutes later. We share a nice meal and then I clean up the kitchen. As I'm drying the last dishes, I hear the front door open. The devil herself has returned.

Lisa goes straight upstairs and it's not long before I hear them arguing.

"Don't lie to me, Lisa," Kevin says. "I know that something went on in this house today."

"You're trippin' right now," Lisa says. "I have no idea what you're talking about."

"Tell me what happened to Amina," Kevin says.

"Why don't you ask her?" Lisa replies.

"I did. She says she fell," Kevin says.

"Well, there you go," Lisa replies.

"I don't believe that shit for a second," Kevin says.

"What do you want me to do, Kevin?" Lisa asks. "I can't babysit Amina, too. She's old enough to take care of herself. If she has a problem putting one foot in front of the other, then it's not my problem. I have enough to worry about with Aaliyah."

"How can you say you watch out for Aaliyah when you're hardly ever here?" Kevin asks. "Besides any of that…what are you doing here right now? Didn't you say that you were leaving and never coming back?"

"I doubt very seriously you were wondering about that last night," Lisa replies snidely.

"Everything with you is sex, sex, sex," Kevin says. "You think you can control me because you're suddenly giving it up again?"

"So now all I'm doing is giving it up?" Lisa asks.

"What do you wanna call it?" Kevin asks. "It's obvious you don't love me. This is a relationship of convenience for you."

"Whatever, nigga," Lisa replies. "You never give me the credit I deserve. All you do is bitch, bitch, bitch. Why don't you just man up?"

"I'll man up when you stop acting so masculine and let me wear the pants around here," Kevin says. "Did you hit Amina?"

"She told you she fell, didn't she?" Lisa says. "And you can wear whatever you want. That don't mean shit to me. I have to be the one in charge. You wouldn't know how to."

"Have you forgotten that this is my house? I take charge whenever I see fit in my own house. So stop acting like you're in control. You want to be in control, start paying for things around here!"

"Whatever," Lisa says. "You're blowing my fucking shit, yo. And you're giving me a headache. Why don't you just quiet the fuck down already? Who needs this drama anyway when Aaliyah is trying to sleep?"

"And why is it that we're always having conversations late at night?" Kevin asks. "And when did you get such a foul mouth? You show up late every night and you never tell me where you've spending all your time. I don't know what you've been doing."

"Oh my God," Lisa says. "Here we go again."

"Don't give me that shit," Kevin replies. "I'm thinking about telling you to go back where you came from."

"You're like a gnat just buzzing around my ear," Lisa says.

"Keep playing me for a joke…" Kevin says. "You already got one foot out the door…"

"I want to get some sleep," Lisa says. "Can't you just argue later? This isn't getting us anywhere."

"God, I wish you didn't come back and just stayed where you were!" Kevin says. "I'm tired of you tempting me with the prospect of you leaving and never coming back. I'll be glad when that happens for real."

"Whatever, nigga!" Lisa says. "I'm done talking to you for real. You're going to have to argue with yourself now."

Kevin

Lisa turns her back and ignores me. Before long, she's sound asleep and breathing heavily.

I hate how I allow her to run all over me the way she does. And why? Because she gives me sex.

Amina, on the other hand, works hard seven days a week, never complains and never demands anything in return.

How could Lisa even part her lips to mention worrying about Aaliyah? What does she do for my daughter? Nothing!

And where the hell is she all day? She doesn't contribute a thing to this house, unless having a bad attitude could be considered a contribution.

Whether Lisa knows it or not, I'm going old school and looking out the front door.

CHAPTER FOURTEEN

Stand Up For Your Rights

Amina

It's been a couple of days since my run-in with Lisa, and I've had the chance to think about it. To be honest, I feel embarrassed now. I should have defended myself. I should not have covered for her. I should have told Kevin the truth.

I have to get out of this house before Lisa kills me. She's violent in addition to being mean. I do not understand what Kevin sees in her. She abuses him, too. Her sex game can't be all that great to make up for how ugly a person she is on the inside. I have never met anyone as selfish as she is.

I feel like crying. I want Alou. He was so sweet to me. He had such plans for us. He's got to be out there some-where. If only I could use the phone. If only I had some money of my own!

My only currency at the moment, though, is to take Salima's advice. I'm beginning to see that she might be right about Kevin. He does seem to be interested in me. Still, I believe that he was just being a good Samaritan. And Lisa does have some power over him. She is ringing his bell every night, after all.

This can't be a contest between me and her but that is what Salima is saying without coming right out and saying it. Maybe she's right.

* * * *

It's time for me to get ready to pick Aaliyah up from school. As I'm freshening up with a blast of Listerine, the phone rings. I check the caller ID and see that's it's Kevin.

"Hello, Kevin," I say after spitting out the mouthwash.

"What are you doing?" Kevin asks.

"Oh, I was just getting ready to walk out the door to get Aaliyah," I reply. "Don't worry. You don't have to check on me. I would never leave your daughter hanging."

"I'm not worried," Kevin says. "I know how responsible you are. I just wanted to catch you before you left. Wait for me. We'll pick her up together."

"I don't know, Kevin," I say. "I still have clothes in the dryer. I…"

"Will you please relax?" Kevin says. "It's not like the world is going to turn on its side if it takes you a couple of hours longer to fold the clothes and put them away. I'll pick you up in a few minutes."

"OK," I reply hesitantly. "But I don't like it."

"Alright, neat freak," Kevin clowns. "I'm hanging up now!"

I wonder what Lisa will do if she comes home and finds no one's here. I'm sure it's not going to be pretty. Yet how can I refuse the man who is in the position to have me deported?

Lisa

I walk in the house and check the rooms. No one's here and I am pissed.

"Where the fuck is that bitch?" I ask myself. "I thought I made myself perfectly clear when I told her about Aaliyah. She'd better back the fuck off!"

I glance down at the cocktail table and see a piece of paper. *What's this?*

I pick up a note from Amina.

> Hi Lisa,
> I'm sorry that we aren't here but Kevin
> called and said he wanted me to go with
> him to the salon so Aaliyah could get her
> hair done. I didn't want you to worry. I
> told Kevin that I wasn't fond of the idea.
> I said I wanted to stay and finish drying
> and folding the clothes. But you know

how he gets. He's so stubborn. He made
me go. It's not my fault. I did try to stay
here and finish my work.
Amina

I'm fuming. That bitch thinks I'm stupid! Well, I'm going
to go give her the surprise of her life!

I grab my purse and head out to the salon.

* * * *

"Where the fuck is that bitch?" I yell as I rush into the
salon.

"Who are you talking about?" Salima asks. "And why
are you using that language in the salon?"

"By the salon, do you mean my man's salon?" I ask
snidely. "And of course we both know that anything his is
mine, so…"

"Let's not go there again," Salima says. "We already
know where that conversation is going to land you. And
since I'm a caring person, sort of like a humanitarian, I
don't want you to embarrass yourself."

"Whatever," I say vehemently. "I don't have time for
you. Where the fuck is Amina with my daughter?"

"I think that Amina is in her skin," Salima says. "And
isn't Aaliyah Kevin's daughter?"

I can't stand this bitch, I think.

"Why are you sweating her, anyway?" shouts one of the

African bitches.

"You need to just leave her the hell alone!" shouts another. "Your problem is with Kevin not Amina. Don't be jealous because you know he's tired of your raggedy ass."

"You wish!" I say confidently. "I have no problem taking care of my man."

"Then why are you here worrying about Amina?" Salima asks.

I want to just line up all of these bitches and smack the shit out of them.

"Mind your own fucking business!" I snap.

"See, that's where you're wrong," Salima says. "When you start fucking with one of us, it is undoubtedly all our business. You need to worry about what would happen to you if I take the leash off of some of my stylists here. It's not going to be pretty if you keep fucking with Amina. To put it bluntly, it will be a problem. But it won't be just anybody's problem, it will be your problem."

"Whatever! I don't have time for this shit!" I snap. "Just tell that bitch to remember I told her not to play with me!"

"Some people have to learn the hard way," says another of these African whores.

"Yadda, yadda, yadda," I reply as I walk out.

****

I head back to the house. I hate when I feel like people are playing games with me.

I pace back and forth in the kitchen, steaming. When I finally look at my watch, I realize that I've wasted a hour and a half.

"You know what?" I say to myself. "I tried to be nice but you can't be nice to niggas, especially African niggas!"

I head out the door with revenge on my mind. There is only one way to quench my thirst and settle this score.

****

"What made you come back today?" Malik asks. "And why are you acting so nice? You were trippin' when I asked you for some earlier."

"That's because you used to look out for me but you don't anymore," I reply, trying to hide the fact that I'm up to something.

"What about what you used to do for me?" Malik asks. "We used to fuck every day. Now you hardly ever give me any."

"Is that all I'm about for you? A piece of ass?" I ask.

"Don't beat me over my head with the bullshit," Malik says. "We both know what it is. Or at least I thought we both knew what it was. I offered to wife you but you weren't with that. You still came around, though, and fucked the shit out of me like it wasn't no thing. So, we both know that we have a give and take relationship. Shit's been a little light for you because that's the way you've been treating me."

"How about I treat you better if you treat me better?" I ask seductively.

"You must want something," Malik says. "You're a piece of shit. The only time you're worried about making me happy is when I give you something."

"That's not true," I say. "I thought we were cool. I thought we were friends. I thought we were supposed to be there for each other."

"And just when are you here for me?" Malik asks.

"Don't do that," I say. "I do shit to you that I don't even do to my man."

"Is there a point to all this?" Malik asks.

"You know what, I'm not going to trip about how you're playing me out right now," I say. "Let me just stick to the business at hand. I need a favor. I need a big favor. I have some things I need to deal with so I need some heat."

"Heat? Fuck you mean heat?" Malik asks.

"Malik, you know what I mean," I reply. "I need a heater."

"You're funny as hell," Malik says. "What the hell are you gonna do with a gun? You'll probably end up shooting yourself in the ass."

"Don't underestimate me, Malik," I say. "I know more than you think I do."

"Maybe you do and maybe you don't," Malik says. "But you still haven't answered my question. Why do you need a gun? Who the fuck do you have a beef with?"

"No one," I say. "But I have to protect myself. You have

enemies. I am with you. All you have to do is think about the fact that you want me to fuck the shit out of you, and I'm about to fuck the shit out of you. Not that we're trading things for sex. You know how we do, though."

"Yeah...I know how we do," Malik replies. "It's like that, then?"

"Yeah...it's like that," I say.

"Well, if it's like that, like you say, and you want something from me, then why is it you still have all your fucking clothes on?" Malik asks me.

Instantly, I get naked and follow through with my promise. But truthfully, since I've been giving Kevin more sex lately, I feel a little guilty about being with Malik.

Fuck it.

Kevin is my man, Aaliyah is my daughter, and that's all anyone needs to know. I know it, all those African bitches at the salon know it, and Kevin knows it. It's gonna be just like it was before Amina's scheming ass came along.

Malik is never gonna know, though. I'm not worried about him. I'm Kevin's and always will be. That man is crazy about me. I'll be damned if I'm going to let Amina take him away from me.

CHAPTER FIFTEEN

Aaliyah – Lisa or Amina?

Kevin

I love spending time with Amina. I don't even think about the age difference anymore. She's mature and responsible. Age ain't nothing but a number anyway.

Amina. I have to be honest. She's all up in my head lately. But why wouldn't she be? She cooks for me, she cleans my house, she washes my clothes, and she takes care of my daughter as if she were her own.

It's unsettling how Lisa says Aaliyah is her daughter. I've never asked Aaliyah how she feels about it since I'm scared of what she might say. But her body language tells me that she's not feeling Lisa like she's feeling Amina.

It's been hard for my baby growing up without a mother. I've tried to give her enough love for two parents but sometimes I don't feel it's enough. Aaliyah never seems completely happy. The happiest I've ever seen her, though, has been since Amina came into our lives.

I sometimes try to imagine our lives if my wife hadn't died giving birth to Aaliyah. I wonder sometimes how Aaliyah would be if Amina was no longer here. Would she ever be happy again?

"Did you have a good time, baby?" I ask my daughter when we pull up to the house.

"Yes, Daddy. I love you," Aaliyah says. "And I love my hair."

"That's good to know," I say to my grown up little girl. "I'll be back in a little while. You go on in with Amina. I'll see you later."

Amina

I don't like what Salima told me about Lisa. I'm glad we arrived after she left. It would have been terrible if Aaliyah had seen Lisa acting crazy like that. All I know is that I'm tired of Lisa bullying me. It's time to stick up for myself.

As I expected, when we come home we find Lisa lounging on the couch, looking like the wicked witch of the east. Not surprisingly, Aaliyah shoots past her like a bat out of hell and runs upstairs to her room.

Lisa is livid. She expects to be treated like Aaliyah's mother. Lisa gives me an icy stare. I don't look away as I've done in the past.

"I know what you're trying to do, bitch," Lisa hisses,

"but I'll deal with you later. Right now I have bigger fish to fry."

I ignore Lisa's comment and watch her run up the stairs. When the coast is clear, I tiptoe halfway up to eavesdrop.

"What's wrong with you, you little bitch?" Lisa asks Aaliyah. "Why do you have an attitude with me? I know that African whore put you up to this and told you not to speak to me. I won't tolerate this attitude from you anymore. Do you hear me?"

I don't hear Aaliyah's answer.

"I'm going to fix this shit right now," Lisa snarls. "I don't want to see you with Amina anymore."

I can't endure what Lisa is doing a minute longer. I climb the rest of the stairs and head into Aaliyah's room.

"Look, Lisa, this is wrong," I say, finally releasing my pent up frustrations. "I have never disrespected you in any way. Since I've come into this house, I've been nothing but nice to you. But you have not returned those sentiments. I've never called you names but all I hear is African bitch this and African bitch that. Everything is attitude with you." I say as I motion for Aaliyah to come to me.

Aaliyah comes close enough for me to grab her. I pick her up and run down the stairs.

"I don't want you to be around Aaliyah anymore," I say forcefully. "Especially not if you're going to call her hideous names."

"Don't you fucking tell me how to raise my daughter!"

Lisa screams as she's running behind me. "You need to re-member that you're a guest in this house. You don't run shit here. I can erase your ass from this equation faster than a math teacher if you don't fall back and collect yourself. I'm the head bitch in charge of shit in this house and you're a nobody. Now give me my daughter!"

Lisa grabs one of Aaliyah's arms and tries to take her away from me. I have her other arm and I'm not letting go. We commence a tug of war with the little girl who may hold both of our fates in her little hands.

"Owww! You're hurting me!" Aaliyah screams. "Let me go!"

Unfortunately, Kevin walks in at that exact moment and hears Aaliyah cry out.

"What the hell is going on in here?" Kevin asks angrily.

"Kevin, you know that I've been nothing but accommo-dating and nice to Lisa. But I will not stand idly by when she calls Aaliyah a little bitch," I say emotionally. Real tears fall from my eyes.

"And I know you're not going to sit here and listen to this nonsense," Lisa tells Kevin. "Your little girl is not sup-posed to listen to our grownup conversations. When we're talking, I told her she needs to make herself scarce."

"I don't know what's going on with either of you, and at the moment, I don't care," Kevin hisses. "Right now I want to know why the two of you were hurting my daugh-ter! She's not some rag doll."

"I'm sorry, Kevin. I got caught up in the moment," I

say. "Lisa is an animal. I had to get Aaliyah away from her abuse."

"Bitch, I'm about to abuse you," Lisa snaps.

"Lisa, I told you about using language like that in my house!" Kevin snaps. "Control yourself!"

"She can't control herself," I say, frustrated. "She's incorrigible!"

"You're just going to let her stand here and talk about me like that?" Lisa asks.

"Talk about you?" Kevin snaps. "Lisa, you are so selfish, it's unbelieveable! We are talking about Aaliyah!"

"Selfish?" Lisa asks. Kevin ignores her.

"And Amina! I'm surprised at you!" Kevin says to me, hurting me deeply. "Lisa may be older than you but I expected you to be the adult. In this situation. In *all* situations. Lisa's immaturity is why I depend on you."

"Immaturity? Now you're saying I'm immature?" Lisa asks angrily.

"Yes, Lisa. Aaliyah is more mature than you," he says. "Aaliyah, honey, go put your shoes on."

"But, Daddy, I was getting ready to watch..." Aaliyah starts to say.

"Go! Now!" Kevin demands.

Aaliyah runs upstairs, slips on her shoes, and is back in a flash. Without saying another word, he glares at us and takes his daughter's hand. We watch as they go out the door.

Instead of jumping on me, Lisa turns and goes upstairs.

I think she's beginning to see that it's not going to be easy for her anymore. Kevin has finally seen her true colors.

Yet my heart sinks. I am all too aware that despite the turmoil Lisa has caused, she'll sleep on a comfortable bed tonight and I'll fall asleep with one eye open on a couch in a living room that does not belong to me.

Lisa has the upper hand. Kevin may not know that she does, but she does. I worry about what she is next going to do to me. No doubt she's going to make my life miserable. Even if she doesn't feel real confident about Kevin right now, I know she'll be scheming as soon as the bedroom door closes. She'll have Kevin on his back in no time, doing what she does. Then she'll blame everyone but herself for her problems. I've learned that about Americans, especially blacks born in America. Nothing is ever anyone's fault. It's always this person's or that person's fault. Or the Man's. I'm still trying to figure out who exactly the Man is.

I take a deep breath and shut the lights before curling up on the couch. I try to relax and breath evenly but tears threaten to spill from my eyes. If only I had someplace else to go, I would leave right now and never look back.

It's sounds like part of the house has fallen down and I jump up grabbing my chest. But it's only Lisa blasting her music at full volume. She's trying to chase her blues away with a bottle of liquor and rap. I know she's trying to drown out the thoughts in her head as well.

Oh, Lord! Will Kevin ever realize that he can do better than Lisa? She is not good for him...nor for his daughter.

Lisa isn't good for anybody. I hope he wakes up before it's too late.

CHAPTER SIXTEEN

Sunday Drama

Lisa

I'm not happy that my man is gone and I'm stuck in this house with that African bush bitch. She's ruined everything! My life was perfect before she came along. I hate her ass! But it's not all her fault. Not even my music can drown out that thought. I blame Kevin, too. Man, do I have some choice words for him when he gets his ass home.

Speak of the devil. I perk up when our bedroom door opens. I turn off the radio and sit up in bed.

"Where have you been?" I demand.

"Don't start with me, Lisa," Kevin says.

"So let me find out you're not speaking to me!" I screech.

"Aaliyah?" Kevin says.

"Hi," Aaliyah says weakly as she peeks into the room.

"Why don't you go on to bed now. Lisa and I have to

129

talk."

"OK, Daddy. 'Night," she says and closes the door behind her.

I start right in on him. "If you would have been listening to me, your woman, instead of that African hoochie, you would have known she's what the problem was all about," I wave after Aaliyah. "I told her not to come into this house without acknowledging my presence. That African whore told her not to…"

"I'm done with that topic," Kevin interrupts me. "You need to drop it."

"I can't just drop it, Kevin," I say. "I'll drop it after you tell me how come you didn't stand up for me when that whore was talking slick? How come you let her disrespect me like that?"

Kevin

I'm amazed at Lisa's one-sided view of things but I know I shouldn't be. I mean, seriously. I walk in the door of my own house where Lisa doesn't pay for a single thing and I find my daughter crying because she's part of a situation that's really all my fault. I don't know why I ever let Lisa feel like she had so much power.

Her speeches go on and on and on with no apparent end in sight, or point for that matter. Why haven't I been able to see the forest from the trees until just recently?

After we got to my mother's, I asked Aaliyah point blank how she feels about both Lisa and Amina. Although she's only a little girl, her genuine words left no room for doubt.

"I love spending time with Amina, Daddy," Aaliyah said. "She talks to me, and she listens to me. Amina always makes sure that I'm OK, " she said. "Lisa just makes me feel like she's the boss of me and that's it. I don't think she cares about me at all. I think all she cares about is being able to tell me what to do and to yell at me."

Noticing my discomfort, my child had the compassion to try to comfort me.

"I'm sorry, Daddy," Aaliyah said. "I didn't start out not liking Lisa. I really tried to like her and I wanted her to like me. But she doesn't like me. That's why I stopped liking her, Daddy. But if you want me to start liking her again, I'll try. I'd do it for you, Daddy. I'd do anything for you. I love you. You're my hero."

Those were the sweetest words I think a child has ever said to a parent. My baby almost had me in tears. But I still had to set her straight.

"Aaliyah, baby, I love you more than anything in this world," I told her. "You don't ever have to like somebody just because you think I would want you to. Yes, you're a little girl but even little girls deserve respect. I'm not going to use grownup words that you won't understand. But I will say that I will never let anyone disrespect you again. And I apologize for allowing it to happen in the first place."

Under the observation of my mother who was peering in from the other room, my daughter and I hugged. I looked up at her over Aaliyah's shoulder and saw her solemnly nod her head just once. That helped me to resolve to make a change in our lives — a change for the better.

****

"Kevin! Answer me!" Lisa screams, shaking me from my thoughts.

"Woman, what are you babbling about now?" I ask.

"Oh, so now I'm babbling?" Lisa asks. "Now you're saying I'm babbling? This little African bitch has thrown a wrench in everything."

"Stop blaming her, Lisa," I argue. "Start taking some responsibility. If you were doing what you were supposed to be doing in this relationship, maybe you'd have no reason to be so insecure."

"Now I'm insecure?" Lisa says. "You were the one who was always making me feel like I was under constant surveillance and scrutiny."

"Was, Lisa, was," I say. "Why are we sitting here arguing? Didn't you say you were leaving and never coming back?"

"Is that it, Kevin? You want me to leave?" Lisa asks. "You want me to leave so that you, Aaliyah and that African bitch can be one big happy family?"

"I'm just tired of your drama, Lisa," I say. "I'm tired of

you calling Amina a bitch when it is very clear to me that you are the bitch. I'm tired of wondering where you are when I call the house during the day. I'm tired of you never answering your cell phone. I'm tired of buying you clothes and you never cooking me meals. Not once have you cooked for me, not once. And I'm tired of you not trying to bond with my daughter. You treat her like a peasant on some assembly line and not your future stepchild."

"Where is all of this coming from, Kevin?" Lisa asks. "Seriously, where is all of this coming from?"

For the first time since I've known her, Lisa actually sounds sincere. She isn't yelling or arguing. She sounds like she's really pained by what I've said and interested in why I feel the way I feel.

"I admit, Kevin, that I haven't been the perfect girl-friend," Lisa says. "And I know I've been far from the perfect fiancée. But you have to admit that I have been trying lately. Think about it, Kevin. Haven't things been getting better between us? The only thing that bothers me now is Amina. I swear she's the only thing. And I promise that once she's out of this house, the changes I need to make, I'll make. But you haven't told me when she'll be leaving. Can you tell me that she'll be leaving in two weeks? A month? Two months? How long is one woman supposed to live in a house with another woman who's not even related? This situation is driving me crazy, Kevin! How much more of this do you think I can take? Baby, how much more of this do you want me to take?"

Lisa slumps down on the bed and cries real tears. For the first time, I start to look at things from her perspective. Maybe I never looked at things that way before. But I can't make this about Lisa.

"Lisa, I know this is an awkward time for me to be asking," I say, "but do you love me?"

Lisa looks me squarely in the eye. ""Yes, Kevin, I love you. I love you so much and I'm scared I'm losing you."

I realize that this is all I've ever wanted to hear Lisa say — for a very long time. But the timing is all wrong.

"Lisa, why couldn't you have told me all this a month ago? Six months ago? A year ago?" I ask.

"Does it make a difference about a month ago or a year ago?" Lisa asks. "I'm telling you I love you right now. The fact that you haven't said that you love me back is scaring me."

"Lisa, I do love you," I admit.

Lisa smiles and perks up. But what I say next brings her right back down.

"But I'm no longer in love with you."

"What?" Lisa says, looking amazed.

"We've been through too much."

"Kevin, everything was fine before Amina came here," Lisa says.

By saying Amina's name, I can tell that she's speaking from her heart and not from the angry place where most of her words normally originate.

"Kevin, I see the way you look at her," Lisa continues.

"I hear how you're always complimenting her and thanking her."

"What am I supposed to say about that? I shouldn't? The fact is that I wanted you to take it upon yourself to care for Aaliyah and me without me having to tell you," I say. "When Amina first came here, her days were numbered. To be truthful, I had hoped another woman in the house would make you step up and treat us like we really were your husband and daughter. But you pushed all your responsibilities as my wife off on Amina. Do you hear me, Lisa? I prayed that you would take care of us like Amina does but you didn't step up."

"Baby, I'm not a homemaker. You knew that going in," Lisa says. "But I was stepping up a little at a time. I would have gotten better. These things take time."

"Are you saying this now because you believe you've run out of time?" I ask. "I've talked to you about stuff like this on many occasions. I know that things take time. Sure. But how much time was I supposed to give you to prove to me that you really care about us?"

"Are you really saying, Kevin, that I'm running out of time?" Lisa asks.

"Lisa, what do you want me to do with these linens?" Amina asks, appearing out of nowhere. "Do you want me to change your sheets or are you going to do it?"

"Amina, please," Lisa says loudly but more out of fear than disrespect. "Kevin and I are talking about something very important."

"Oh, I'm sorry," Amina apologizes and disappears. A glimmer of love and satisfaction fill me. I try to hide my feelings but I don't think I did a good job of it.

Lisa watches me intently. "Well, I think the answers to my questions are written all over your face," Lisa says.

"Lisa, you don't know how much I would have appreciated *you* if only you would have really shown me that you wanted to take care of me and my daughter," I say.

"This isn't happening to me," Lisa says softly. Then, "This isn't fucking happening to me!" she screams loud enough to blow the roof right off the house.

"Lisa, remember Aaliyah's sleeping," is all I can say.

Lisa

"How do you expect me to feel, Kevin?" I ask. "Everything we had is slipping away."

"It's everything we had but, really, is it everything you've wanted?" Kevin asks me.

"How can you sit here and tell me what I wanted?" I ask loudly.

"You never made me feel secure, Lisa," Kevin says. "I always felt like you could be here today and gone tomorrow."

"Who's acting like they're gone?" I ask. "Kevin, ever since that bitch moved in here…" I say with a sigh.

"I didn't have any intentions, if that's what you think,"

Kevin interrupts.

"Come on!" I reply. "You have a salon full of African bitches. Our biggest disagreements are about African bitches. It's so perfect that one of them would end up the source of our drama now. The salon wasn't good enough for you! You had to move one of them into our house!"

"Lisa, what about you?" Kevin asks. "Are you saying you did everything the exact way you were supposed to?"

"Of course I didn't and of course you didn't," I reply. "But I'm not the one sitting here telling you that you ran out of time. I'm not the one with an African bush bitch fetish. Having them in the salon wasn't good enough. You had to get one for the house! She's not drapery, Kevin. You can't decorate the house with her just to make yourself feel better. You have a woman. You can't be so naïve to think that you can force your woman to accept another woman living in her own house! And why the hell does it have to be an African woman? You never want to admit it but we both know that's your thing."

"I didn't want to go there, Lisa, but since you did…," Kevin says. "You say I forced you to accept another woman staying in my house, but you never came clean about when you walked out of our neighbor's house. You think I can't find things out, Lisa? I know that your ex-boyfriend hangs out there. And don't try to convince me that you two are just friends," Kevin says.

My mouth falls wide open. I didn't expect this.

"OK. If you need to hear it, Kevin, I fucked him," I

admit. "Yes, I fucked him. But it's not like I was into him. I talked to you all the time and you never listened to me. I was paying you back for fucking all those African bitches in your salon."

"Don't put this on me, Lisa! I never fucked any of my workers. Nor would I," Kevin responds.

"Yeah, right," I reply. "My ears are to the street. Everybody talks about the private massages that go on there. Everybody in Harlem knows it's not just a hair spot. It's a fuck spot. You cannot tell me that you didn't join in the fun."

"I never fucked anybody else while I've been with you, Lisa," Kevin says. "Not even once. You were all the woman I needed."

"Stop fucking lying, Kevin!" I snap. "Keep it fucking real. I thought we were having an honest conversation right now."

"You may be keeping it real by admitting that you fucked outside of this relationship. But don't try to tell me I'm lying when I say that I didn't," Kevin says. "If you thought I was sleeping around on you – wrong! If you did for pay back – wrong again. I loved you more than I ever thought it was possible for me to love another woman."

"What's up with the past tense, Kevin?" I ask. "Hmm? What's up with the past tense?"

"I already told you that I still love you," Kevin says. "What the hell do you want from me?"

"Everything, Kevin," I say. "I want everything."

"I'm sorry, baby, but it's over," Kevin says. "We've been through too much. There are too many bruises in our relationship to heal."

I lose it.

I seem to step outside of myself and lift off of the bed. I knock everything off the dressers, throw glasses. I rip the sheets of the bed, throw pillows at him, throw anything I can get my hands on. My tirade lasts a long time. I don't know how long.

When the dust and I settle, I see I've made a wreck of the place. I hear Aaliyah crying, and Kevin is looking at me like I'm a certifiable. I feel so disrespected by that look coming from a man who chased me forever and a day. What the fuck does he mean he's breaking up with me? And how dare he look at me like I'd go crazy over the fact that he's breaking up with me.

"You win, Kevin," I finally say. "If this is what you want, you win. But I guarantee you that African bitch won't."

CHAPTER SEVENTEEN

Malik, the Thug

Lisa

It's midnight when I leave Kevin's house and hop into my
SUV. I turn on the tunes. My mind is racing a mile a
minute. I'm formulating a plan but I need money. With the
debit card Kevin gave me, I withdraw the maximum
amount I can. I plan to wipe that nigga out!

Where else is there for me to go but to Malik's? Part of
me hates him because he's the reason I had to go into rehab
in the first place. But the sexual chemistry between us is un-
deniable. I go to him because I'm hooked on him. And I
can't front, I like getting high. What's the problem with a
couple of hits every once in a while? Or every day? I can
handle my addictions. My problems at home disappear for a
while and isn't that better than thinking about them all the
time? Fucking Malik, that's just icing on the cake.

Malik's become one of the biggest drug lords in

Harlem. When people need weight in powder, they run to him just like I do. But this time, I don't need Malik for that. I need to draw the final line in the sand between that bitch and me, and Malik is gonna help me — even if he's unaware that he's helping me.

Kevin owes me. I surrender my heart to him, tell him my true feelings, and he kicks me out? He has the game fucked up!

I'll let him mourn a little. Then I'll step right back in to where I left off. Who's gonna miss that African bitch anyway?

****

Almost every morning after I take the maximum I can out of the bank, I swing by Kevin's and park down the street. I watch as Amina takes Aaliyah to school and wait for her to get back. She goes out more often now. I follow her when she goes shopping and when she stops in the salon. A couple of times, I think she sees me. But I roll up the tinted windows and peel away. She's so naïve, she's got no idea I'm spying her.

Almost a month has gone by and Kevin is thousands of dollars poorer. I've also managed to convince Malik to get me a gun, for my own protection. I can't be hanging out with a drug lord and not have some heat is what I told him. But never in my wildest dreams did I think that Malik would make me sex him for so damned long before giving in.

He thinks we're a couple now. It baffles me how he's come to that conclusion after all the times I told him that I didn't see him like that. I call him Vegas, like in Las Vegas. It's a fun place and you enjoy it when you're there. But who really wants to live there?

Malik knows that I don't want a drug dealer as my man. He refuses to believe that it's true, however. I guess with me fucking him every day, he would see things that way. True, we've been spending a lot of time together. But when I leave him, I pretend I'm going back to Kevin's. I haven't told him we broke up. Let him be ignorant. He doesn't know I go to Michelle's most nights and hotels if it gets too late to show up on her tight ass door.

The drama of him is behind me now. I got what I need — a Smith and Wesson Desert Eagle Colt 45.

****

Feeling the heat in my hand helps me get my stalk on. I park across the street from *my* home and curse myself for leaving it in the first place. Kevin really should have stuck up for me with that African whore. He's gonna regret his decision.

But no. I love him. He will be my life. Him and that bratty little bitch of a daughter. Amina? It's all her fault She's gonna pay for what she's done to me.

****

I wait for hours. Where can they be on a Friday evening?

I decide to head over to the salon and do some negotiating. I know Salima can't stand me, and I ain't feelin' her that much either. But one thing I do know about Africans is that they love money more than anything in the world. Friendship is supposed to mean a lot, but I feel confident that Salima will be more interested in me greasing her palms than remaining loyal to someone she hasn't known very long.

As expected, Salima rolls her eyes at me when I enter the salon. I'm not dismayed, though. I walk over to her station and start talking.

"I'm looking for Kevin. I know he's with that bitch. I need you to tell me where they went."

"You don't need me to do shit," Salima declares emphatically. "When did we become fly like that?"

"We don't have to be fly," I say. "You do something for me and I'll do something for you."

"What can you do for me besides getting the hell out of my face and stop sucking up all of my good air?" Salima asks.

"Come on now. Whether you like me or not, you know I'm not a stupid person," I say. "What else would I come to you with other than money? You're human like anyone else. And you may just love money more than anyone I know. I know you have a price."

"A price for what?" Salima asks.

I can see her bending already and I haven't even put in all that much effort.

"I'll give you five hundred dollars if you tell me where they are," I say. "It's Friday evening and although Kevin doesn't check in on a lot of nights, I know for a fact that he's been checking in today. Friday is a big money day. You know damned well he's called you at least a dozen times today."

"You're funny," Salima says. "I guess you do know him well. He was your man, after all. Emphasis on the word *was*."

"I don't have time for games," I respond. "Five hundred bucks for some information. So, where they at?"

"I can't front. I don't like you, Lisa," Salima says. "But right now, you're pitiful. I don't think you want to do this to yourself. Kevin is about to marry Amina. We both can see the way he feels about her. He plans to make her an honest woman so she can stay in this country. Furthermore, Aaliyah loves Amina. And she deserves a good mother. Why don't you do everyone and yourself a favor and leave it alone. Walk out this door with your dignity and don't ever come back. Forget about Kevin. He's a lost cause."

I see that Salima is delighted with herself for having en-lightened me. She smiles widely as if to twist the knife a lit-tle bit more. I can't be moved though. I remain focused on the task at hand.

"In that case," I say, "I'll give you a thousand dollars.

It's not going to hurt you any. And you'll go home a lot richer than you would have. You won't even have to steal out of the till tonight," I tell her. Since Salima's throwing blows, I'm happy to throw one of my own.

"I guess you like torturing yourself," Salima says with a devious smile. "Give me the money and I'll let you know where they are."

Suspicious, I reach into my purse and peel off a thousand from the three thousand dollar knot I was prepared to part with for the information. Slowly, I hand her the money.

"Relax," Salima says. "I'm not going to fuck you. When it comes to my money, I'm a very honest person. I always try to make sure that people doing business with me walk away feeling like they've gotten their money's worth."

"Save the bullshit, Salima, and just tell me what I need to know," I say, becoming irked.

"Kevin dropped his daughter off at his mother's. He and Amina are out for a romantic dinner," Salima says. "They went to an African restaurant about five blocks from here. I believe he's going to tell her that he wants to marry her tonight. It'll be a special night for them. Amina may finally give him some."

"Whatever," I snap, not hiding how irritated I am about the situation.

I turn to walk out. I don't have as much time as I thought I had to put an end to this nonsense.

"Let me know when you want to do some more business," Salima calls out from behind me. "I'm a plethora of information."

I ignore her and keep it moving. This is one battle I don't plan on allowing Amina to win.

CHAPTER EIGHTEEN

African Restaurant

Amina

My life has been so much more pleasant since Lisa's been gone. Kevin, Aaliyah and I are like a real family. Kevin has started giving me a weekly allowance of two hundred dollars, as well. I want so badly to repay him for what he's done for me that I decided to take him out to dinner.

"Amina, this place is wonderful!" Kevin says. "But you didn't have to do this. Let me take care of the bill. I don't want you spending your money. I want you to do something special for yourself instead."

"Nonsense," I protest and lean over to kiss him on the lips. "You are my knight in shining armor. And this is not a one-sided relationship. We do things for each other. Now, do you know what you want to eat?"

"Why don't you order for us?" Kevin suggests. "I'm kind of out of my element here. You know what I like and you understand the menu. I'm sure you won't steer me wrong."

"OK, then," I say happily. "I'll order us the spicy chicken with gravy over rice, fried plantains and steamed vegetables."

"Sounds good to me," Kevin says as the waitress approaches and takes our order.

As we wait to be served, we talk happily about our day and Aaliyah. Life couldn't be any more perfect.

"Oh my God!" I say aloud.

At that moment, Lisa comes through the door and walks right towards us. Seems I may have spoken too soon.

Lisa

"Kevin, get your fucking ass up and let's go," I shout angrily. "Don't make me fucking embarrass you in this place."

"What do you mean? You have already embarrassed me," Kevin says. "I am not leaving. We've already ordered. What are you doing here?"

"You're not to be asking any questions," I respond as I throw two twenties on the table. "Now your food is paid for. They don't give a shit if you eat it or not. Now, let's be out like I said. Don't make me get fucking ignorant."

"You're already are ignorant," a patron of the restaurant says behind me.

I recognize her to be one of the bitch customers from

the salon.

"You need to mind your fucking business," I say. "And trust me, it won't be a good look for you if I go over there and fuck around. Focus on your table and your shit. Let me worry about what's going on over here. If you interrupt me again, believe me, it's going to be a problem."

"Lisa, what are you doing?" Kevin asks. "You've left me I don't know how many times. You don't really love me. You don't even like my daughter. You know that it won't work between us."

"Don't tell me how I feel about you!" I say forcefully. "And what the hell do you mean that I don't like your daughter? I can see that you've been listening to this hating-ass bitch again."

"Amina doesn't have anything to do with this," Kevin says. "I talked to Aaliyah on my own. She told me herself that she doesn't think you like her."

"This bitch probably coached Aaliyah to say it," I say. "The fact of the matter is that she's still behind it. Open your eyes and see that she's the source of our problems. Everything was perfect until she came along."

"Ma'am, I'm going to have to ask you to leave," the restaurant manager tells me. "I've called the police. They're on their way."

I ignore the him and focus on Kevin. "Don't make me fucking tell you again to leave!" I scream. "I'm about to get real fucking ugly up in here."

During a brief stalemate, the manager leaves and comes

back with the owner. He tries to reason with Kevin.

"Kevin, are you not able to control your female friends?" asks the owner. "You are the man of your home, correct?"

"I am the man in my home and she no longer lives in it," Kevin says. "I just want her to leave us alone."

"I ain't leaving shit alone!" I snap. "You need to leave this African bitch alone!"

The women in the restaurant shoot daggers at me with their eyes. I'm still not moved.

"You need to get over this fascination you have with these bush bitches!" I say angrily to Kevin, not worried if I'm hurting anyone's feelings or being politically correct.

"Kevin! Please!" the owner implores. "Miss, will you please leave my restaurant?" the owner asks me.

"I ain't going no fucking where without him," I say, standing my ground.

"Kevin, walk with me," the owner says.

Kevin gets up and walks with the owner to the door. Of course, I follow. I'm not beat for Amina at all or looking at her ugly face. I really don't understand what Kevin sees in her.

I can hear the patrons whispering about how weak Kevin is because he can't control me. Fuck them! Ain't no nigga never gonna control me!

They may as well mind their own fucking business and leave ours alone. I don't care about nobody else's stupid-ass opinion. I'm good. I can handle my handle on my own.

"Kevin, please, make her leave," the owner pleads.

"He can't make me do shit!" I snap. "Yeah! Uh huh! I'm still fucking here. Little L is in the motherfucking building and like I said I ain't going no fucking place without my man."

"This is getting ridiculous, Kevin," the owner says.

"You're right. I'll talk her outside," Kevin says.

Outside to talk? My ass! I think. *Whether he knows it or not, he's leaving with me.*

Amina

I feel sorry for Lisa. I know how bad it feels to lose a good man. I lost Alou.

I also feel sorry for Kevin. Lisa is an embarrassment. Sure, she probably feels like she's punked me. But it is Kevin, the man she has come to reclaim, who matters. Can she really be crazy enough to think Kevin would take her back after this display?

I'm glad she has shown her true colors. The other Africans in the restaurant keep looking over at me as if to ask *Who is this beast?* I think it's funny in a sad way. How can Lisa do battle with me, the woman who has already won the war?

After she left, I was unsure of what would happen. I hardly spoke to Kevin those first few days after. I wanted to give him the time to feel comfortable with his decision and for Aaliyah to get over the trauma.

But the following week, he came to me and asked me if I would like to sleep in the guest room instead of on the couch. I thanked him politely but was so happy on the inside. His offer of the guest room meant more to me than anything. I suddenly felt safe and secure. I knew then that he would not have me deported.

And for the first time since I came to New York, I decided to forget about looking for Alou. Salima was right about everything — even about me being naïve. The most important thing to Kevin is his daughter and she showed him the path. He took it.

So I am going to eat my food and enjoy myself and forget all about Lisa. Kevin will deal with her.

CHAPTER NINETEEN

Engaged

Amina

Kevin has been doing everything he can to make up for the incident at the restaurant, but I told him it's not necessary. It wasn't his fault. I know how ignorant Lisa is, and I'm not worried about her at all.

So today, he invites Aaliyah and me to Marcus Garvey Park for a picnic. I don't turn him down. Some fresh air and warm sun will be enjoyable. It'll be fun to get out and enjoy the nice weather.

Rather than pick us up, Kevin decides to meet us at the park and tells us to take a cab. I don't question him at all.

I don't have a problem taking cabs or even jumping on the bus. I don't consider myself to be a diva or ghetto fabulous. As long as I have Kevin and Aaliyah in my life, I'm happy. Anything else he decides to do for me, I'll consider it a bonus.

When the taxi drops us off, Aaliyah and I see a sign with our names on it and a big red arrow pointing in the direction we have to walk. I am so excited.

White rose petals line the path we have to take. At the end of the path, a furry, white, bear-shaped blanket is laid out over the grass. Standing in an arc at the edges of the blanket are five men, all of them dressed in white tuxedos and bow ties, their right arms extended. In each hand sits a mammoth white dove.

Behind the five men is a large group of people standing together in white robes. Why they are there instantly becomes apparent. They begin to sing a beautiful ballad I later find out is At Last made famous by the singing legend, Etta James. The words are so beautiful, and the choir sings them so beautifully, I am moved to tears. Honestly, the entire scene is overwhelming and I feel myself becoming extremely emotional.

Just as I wonder where Kevin could be, the choir parts and he emerges. He glides to the beat of the song and heads in our direction. I can't believe how much care and attention to detail Kevin has put into making our picnic special.

Without acknowledging me, he looks at Aaliyah and asks, "Did you bring what I asked you to bring?"

"Yes, sir," Aaliyah tells him.

"OK then. Let's get started!" Kevin announces. He takes Aaliyah's hands in his and pulls her in front of him. They are standing directly in front of me.

"Miss Amina... Mom... Is it alright if I call you Mom?" Aaliyah asks.

I am speechless. Tears threaten to spill down my cheeks. I don't cry, though. I just shake my head to let Aaliyah know that it's OK for her to call me Mom. If she only knew how special asking me that question makes me feel.

"Alright, then, Mom," Aaliyah continues. "I can't remember the last time I've been so happy. You are so nice to me, and I can tell that you really care about me. So I asked my Dad not to be silly and to make you a permanent part of our lives. I brought you something but I can't give it to you. My dad has to give it to you. I hope you accept it."

I'm a little confused as Aaliyah places her little hand in Kevin's. An exchange has been made but I can't imagine what it is. Aaliyah looks up at her father in approval and Kevin begins to speak.

"Amina, sweetheart, if I had prayed a million nights and asked God a million times to send me an angel as perfect as you, I would never have believed that he could. You have made me and my daughter feel important. You take such good care of us. You cook for us when we're hungry, you clean up after us when we're sloppy, and you never complain. Everything you do for us, I know you do it out of love."

"I really love you. Yes," I say. "I love both of you."

"Wait...let me finish," Kevin says. "The most beautiful words I ever heard was when Aaliyah told me how happy you make her and how much she loves you. It made me look into myself and realize how lucky I was to help you that day when you needed your own angel. Helping you, being a good human being and deciding not to turn my back on you in your moment of despair were the smartest things I've ever done."

Kevin shifts his weight nervously from one foot to the other. I find it adorable that he is nervous.

"While taking you into my home was an extremely smart thing to do, I did some stupid things after you settled in. The dumbest of all was to pretend that I didn't care about you as much as I did. I am so sorry for putting you through what you went through with Lisa. I'm sorry that I denied the fact that I truly love you. But now as I look in your beautiful eyes and tell you that I love you, I promise to never let you be unhappy again. I will never let you go. I will try to make you as happy as you've made my daughter and me. For the rest of your life."

Kevin opens his hand and reveals a ring. He grabs my left hand, still looking me squarely in the eye, and says, "Amina, I love you with all of my heart, and I want to spend the rest of my life with you. I want you to be my wife. Will you marry me?"

I am stupefied. I can't believe that this is happening.

My silence becomes deafening for at least one of the three of us. Aaliyah speaks to hurry things along.

"Please say yes, Miss Amina!" Aaliyah pleads. "Please! You said I could call you Mom. Please make it permanent."

"I'm sorry," I say. "I'm just so overwhelmed. That's

why it's hard for me to speak. Yes. Of course yes! I love you both! I'm so happy right now. The two of you have just made me the happiest woman in the world."

Now I let myself cry tears of joy. Kevin and Aaliyah grab me in a group hug. Everything is perfect. Allah has blessed me with this good man and his angel of a daughter. I am so thankful and so happy. A happy future will be Allah's greatest gift to me.

Lisa

So, Salima's information was dead accurate. I may hate the bitch but she has been professional with me in our business dealings.

Through a common acquaintance, she sent me a message to come by the salon. She had some news she knew I'd find very valuable.

Once I got arrived, though, Salima wouldn't budge. "I guarantee you'll want to hear this," Salima said. "But I will not open my mouth for a penny less than five thousand dollars.

"Two thousand?" I asked her.

She shook her head no.

"Twenty-five hundred?"

"NO!"

"Three thousand?"

Still no. Damn!

Finally I said fuck it and agreed to five thousand. "Now, what information is so valuable?"

"I'm not dumb," Salima said. "Put it in my hand."

I gave her the money. She counted it all out and floored me with the next words out of her mouth.

"Two days from now Kevin will be putting a ring twice the size of that one on Amina's finger," Salima informed me as she gestured to my engagement ring.

"You're lying," I replied.

"I know for a fact it's true because someone I'm cool with is in the choir Kevin hired to sing when he proposes to her," Salima said. "That's why I wanted so much money. I'm paying for this information. Well, that's not a hundred percent accurate. The information wasn't that expensive. I charged you up because I don't really like you and I know you don't really like me."

"Will you get on with it?" I demanded. "Neither one of us has time for that type of stuff."

"Yes. Right you are," Salima agreed. "Money talks and bullshit walks. Anyway, I greased a palm and you'll be getting an actual audiotape of the proposal, two days from now at Marcus Garvey. You really don't need to be there. You may just mess things up. But if you need to see it for yourself, go incognito. One o'clock, east end. Believe me when I say that my contact is on point. Come by here after I close on Monday and I'll give you the tape."

* * * *

158

There was no way I'd stay away. As infuriated as I am, I watch from the sidelines as my man proposes to that bitch. All the shit he's done for that bitch, the tuxedos and choir and flowers, is so over the top, I want to get a bucket of red paint and splash it all over them.

I feel like I'm being stabbed in the heart but they need to be the ones bleeding.

Well, there's only one thing left to do and I've been putting it off far too long.

CHAPTER TWENTY

Zoodoo Nightclub

Lisa

"Kevin, I want to celebrate!" Amina's voice rings out clearly from the tape. "Do you think your mom would mind watching her tonight so we can go to Zoodoo?"

"I'm way ahead of you," Kevin says. "I already had a celebration planned. If Zoodoo Nightclub is where you want to go, then Zoodoo Nightclub is what it will be."

"Good! Baby, I love you," Amina says.

When I hear the sound of them kissing, I turn the tape off. I feel like I'm about to throw up in my mouth.

So they think they're going to celebrate tonight? I don't think so. I have something else in mind for them.

* * * *

"Come on, Malik," I plead. "How long has it been since we

went out together? You're always sweatin' me to go out and now that I suggest it, you're not interested."

"But Zoodoo?" Malik says. "That's some African shit. You know I don't really be doing the club thing anyway. But African music? What the fuck am I supposed to do with that?"

"You're supposed to push up on me really close and grind on this big ass," I say seductively while moving my body. "You know how much I like foreplay. Once we get each other all worked up on the dance floor, I guarantee you it'll be a night to remember."

"Is that right?" Malik asks.

Amina

As I show off my engagement ring to my African friends from the salon and the market, I feel like a star. My ring is a three carat diamond, yet it looks perfect on my hand. Truthfully, it could be cubic zirconia and I would still be proud to wear it. It's from Kevin, a sign of his love and devotion, and that's all that I care about.

"Congratulations to Amina and her fiancé, Kevin!" the deejay shouts out through the microphone. "Tonight is their impromptu engagement party. I wish them the best. I hope y'all have lots of kids! I wanna be a godfather!"

After that, people come over to congratulate us. Zoodoo is a meeting place for Africans, many of whom are professionals, and they want to meet Kevin to exchange ideas and network. He doesn't mind. He may even walk away tonight with some new business opportunities.

I, on the other hand, just want to savor the moment. This is the culmination of a long journey that's been filled with pain, frustration, heartache and despair. I close my eyes to the sound of African music and zone out. Tonight is my night and I want to enjoy all the pleasures.

When I open my eyes, I'm looking at a nightmare. Lisa is heading right for us with a guy. Before I know what's happening, Lisa bumps into me hard.

"Dammit you dumb bitch," Lisa snarls. "Why don't you get the fuck out of the way?"

"Lisa? What are you doing here?" Kevin asks when he sees her.

"You know this dude?" Lisa's friend asks.

"This dude is my fiancé," Lisa says.

"Ex-fiancé," I say, correcting Lisa.

I lift up my ring to flash it just in case my words aren't enough.

"I got one of those too, bitch," Lisa says.

She lifts her hand in the air to show off her own ring.

"Huh, it's nowhere near as nice as mine," I say.

Lisa looks like she's about to get physical with me but her friend grabs her. He looks really upset.

"Let me find out that you dragged me down here for this bullshit," Lisa's friend says. "I can't believe you tried to play me."

"Ain't nobody trying to play you," Lisa says. I know she's lying. "This is just a coincidence."

"Coincidence, my ass," her friend says. "You knew they were going to be here. You've been playing me out all along."

"Nobody is playing you, Malik," Lisa says. "I never told you that Kevin and I broke up."

"Oh, so this is Kevin," Malik says. "Now I really know that you're trying to play me. Let's be out, yo. You're on some bullshit."

"Let's be out? We just got here," Lisa says. "We don't have to leave. Besides, look at how little Kevin looks compared to you. I know you ain't scared mister big baller, shot caller."

"Bitch, you know I ain't never been scared of another nigga," Malik says. "But it's obvious that this dude ain't checking for you. You need to get out of here and stop embarrassing yourself. I ain't fucking playing with you. Let's be out now. If you want to stay here and look like a dumb ass do that shit on your own. I can't believe your fucking ass has been playing me the whole time. What part of the fucking game is this?"

"Whatever," Lisa says. "I already told you ain't nobody trying to play you."

Malik pulls on Lisa's arm for a while but gives up. When he sees she isn't going to leave, he leaves alone.

"I'm out, yo," Malik says.

"Whatever," Lisa says. "Later for your lame ass." Lisa

turns towards me. "Now back to your ass."

Before I tell Lisa she'd be better off just leaving, the crowd starts chanting. "Out...out...out..."

"You better listen to them," I say.

"Oh, I'm leaving," Lisa says. "But not before I beat your ass."

Lisa swings and hits me in the face. The blow catches me off guard but this time I don't just accept her hitting me. I swing back and punch her in the face as well.

We square up to do battle but before we can get into it, several African women I know from the salon jump on Lisa.

"Bitch, I've been waiting to dig into your shit," one of them says.

"Hell, yeah! This feels better than Christmas morning," says another as she swings and connects with Lisa's shoulder.

The women pummel Lisa then pick her up and drag her out of the club.

"Hip, hip, hurrah...hip, hip, hurrah...hip, hip, hurrah," the crowd chants.

Once Lisa is gone, I don't give her another thought. I snuggle up next to Kevin with my back to him on the dance floor and grind into him until I feel his nature rising.

He makes me feel sexy. I love knowing that he wants me so badly. I resolve to give him everything he wants just as he's given me all I could ever ask for.

Later on tonight, I'm going to show him that I love him. I close my eyes and visualize our lovemaking as we dance, knowing that in just a few hours our bodies will be as one as we take our relationship to the next level.

CHAPTER TWENTY-ONE

Innocent Victim

Lisa

Malik is outside the club when those African bitches push me out the door and throw me to the ground.

"We never want to see your skanky ass around here ever again, you bitch!" one yells at me.

"Fuck all of you!" I scream back at them.

"Look at you," Malik says.

I turn my head. "Fuck you, too!" I shout at him as I lift myself off the ground. I start to stomp away.

"Now where do you think you're going?" he asks me.

I stop because I have no idea. I can't go to Michelle's looking like a slut who's gotten the shit beat out of her. I'd never hear the end of it.

"Open the fucking door," I tell him.

I feel like shit. Fuck! Things didn't go down the way I thought they would.

"Yeah, you played my ass, Lisa. But you know what, you deserved that ass whuppin'," he tells me.

"What do you know about anything?" I try to yell at him but my jaw hurts so much it comes out like I'm crying.

"Ain't no reason for you to be all nasty to me. Who's here picking you up off the ground?" Malik asks me. "You shoulda told me what was going down instead of playing me for a fool."

"You shouldn't have thought that we were a couple," I respond.

"Why the hell not? You made yourself at home in my place, coming at me every chance you got. Yeah, but I sorta figured you had some other shit going on."

"Malik, stop being so fucking funny and get me cleaned up," I tell him.

We get back to his place and I'm sore as hell. He helps me strip down and makes a warm bath for me. All the while, I'm wondering who the fuck he thinks he is.

After I slide into the tub, he gets a cloth and wipes off my face. I can't see them but I know I have a couple of bruises and at least one black eye. I'm so angry, I want to tell him to stop but I can't.

"Lisa, I get that you want to hurt your ex-fiancé," Malik says with an edge to his voice, "but have you thought about the fact that that nigga just ain't into you no more?"

"What's it to you? He's mine and I want him back," I explain.

"No. You don't want her to have him. That's what's really getting to you," he says. "And now he ain't never gonna be wanting you. You fucked up."

"Again, what is it to you?" I ask him.

"You. You're it to me," he says quietly.

I can't believe what I'm hearing. "You know it ain't like that for us. We just do what we do," I tell him.

Malik's looking at me in a way I've never seen him look at me before. "You think I want you to run off and marry Kevin?"

I think about it.

"See, you don't know how I feel about you. You're so into your own shit!" he says. "I never was playin'. I can't front neither. But you had to go and find out the hard way that Kevin just ain't into you. Damned stubborn bitch!"

Malik grabs a towel off the door and tosses it to me. I get up out of the bath and wrap myself up in it.

"Come here and sit," he says as he points to the toilet. He's closed the lid for me. Then he takes out some cotton balls and hydrogen peroxide from the cabinet and dabs some on the scrapes on my elbows and knees.

"Why you being so fucking nice to me, huh Malik?" I ask him.

"Because I hate your fucking guts," he says with a laugh.

* * * *

It takes a few days to lick my wounds and recover from the

fiasco at the club. I can't front, those African bitches whupped my ass. But I'm not embarrassed. They had to jump me as a group. Not one of them could stand toe to toe with me and take me out. Nevertheless, an ass whupping is an ass whupping and they dug into my shit hard.

Malik's been in and out, doing his thing then buying me medicine and bringing it back. I never saw this side of him before and I'm not loving it. I don't want him the way I want Kevin. I will never want him the way I want Kevin. He's just a means to an end.

Today is another day, though. I'm feeling better and I have my priorities straight. It's time to go out and get what's mine. It's time for payback.

* * * *

I know what time that African whore will arrive to pick up my daughter. So I wait outside the school with the air on and the tinted windows closed.

It's the last week of school and the weather is nice. Yet I'm sitting in the car with a ski mask over my face. It feels good to be so close to reaching my goals. I am stoked, ready to pounce.

While I'm laying in the cut, a taxi pulls up and Amina jumps out. I want to take her out right now but I get the feeling that a better opportunity will present itself. She usually walks the kid to and from school so with her holding the taxi, I see that she has a different plan for this afternoon.

Even better for me. There are too many kids around and I wouldn't want to hurt an innocent kid. I want to get a clean shot.

Some dumb bitch behind me starts blowing her horn. I guess she's trying to rush me to leave. Ordinarily, I would have jumped out of the car and handled the situation but I can't risk blowing my cover. Instead I say 'fuck you' into the rearview mirror.

Fuck! I almost miss seeing Amina and Aaliyah get back into the cab. I pull out of the parking space and follow inconspicuously. I'm not right on top of it but I also don't fall too far behind. I'm hoping they make a detour along the way that suits my purposes.

So I'm thrilled when the taxi pulls up to an African market.

"This bitch ain't about to serve that African bullshit to my daughter!" I say to myself as I roll the window down and brace myself.

The back door opens, streetside, and I start blazing.

Band...bang...bang!

Before anybody realizes what's happening, a bloody body drops to the ground.

Oh shit!

Aaliyah!

I don't stay there and panic. I calmly close the window and pull away before anyone gets a good look at the SUV or the gun smoking on the passenger seat.

* * * *

"Think, bitch, think!" I say to myself as I drive to Malik's.

When Malik gave me the gun, he wasn't wearing gloves. Fool. I had counted on it, though, and every time I handled the gun, without being obvious, I never got my fingerprints on it. Today I wore gloves. So I never touched the gun with my bare hands. Malik did. His fingerprints are all over it. So if any bullshit were to come out of this, the gun couldn't be traced back to me.

Back at Malik's, I hide the S&W where he'll never look. But at the same time, I put it where I believe a cop would look. I've watched enough Law&Order SVU and my favorite, The Wire, to know how cops think.

After hiding the gun, I leave as if nothing ever happened. Then I busy myself acting normal, going places I would normally go to in the afternoon and doing what I would normally do.

Amina

"Oh my God! No!!!!!" I scream hysterically. "Aaliyah, baby, hold on! I'm getting help. Hold on! Helpppppppppp, pleeeeeeeeeeeze, helpppppppppppppp!!! We have to get her to the hospital!"

Frantically, the taxi driver jumps out of the car and helps me put Aaliyah in the back seat. She's so bloody, I can't see where she was shot.

We are racing to the hospital and I do what I dread most. I call Kevin.

Kevin

"Kevin! Oh my God, Kevin!" Amina screams into the phone. "I can't breath. I can't breath. I can't breath!"

Amina's crying. I think she's having a panic attack or a nervous breakdown. "Sweetie, relax. Tell me what's going on," I say.

"Some maniac…some crazy person…it was terrible! I don't believe what happened!" Amina screams.

"You can't believe that what happened, Amina?" I say. "You're scaring me. Is everything OK?"

"No! Everything is far from OK," Amina shrieks. "I'm in a taxi, heading to the hospital. You have to meet me there…"

"Hospital? What happened? What did you do to yourself?" I ask.

"It's not me, it's not me!" Amina cries. "Jah, why did this happen? I wish it was me, oh my God, I swear I wish it was me!"

"You wish what was you, Amina? You're not making sense!" I say as I glance at the time on the dashboard. "What's going on? You didn't forget to pick up Aaliyah from school, did you?"

"I picked her up. Then we went to the market," Amina says. "Oh why didn't I just go straight home?"

"Goddammit, Amina! Tell me what the fuck is going on!" I yell into the phone. Now I'm losing it.

I hear Amina breath really hard and exhale into the phone. "Some crazed, psychotic person started shooting today when we arrived at the market," Amina tells me. "I'm heading to the hospital right now. Aaliyah was hit. It's bad, baby. It's very bad."

"Wait one second," I say nervously. "Are you telling me somebody shot my daughter? Is that what you're saying to me right now?"

"Yes. It happened so fast," Amina says. "She got out of the taxi and I heard gunshots. When I ran around the car to see what happened, she was lying on the ground, bleeding."

"Shit, Amina!" I snap. "What hospital are you going to?"

"We just arrived at Harlem Hospital," Amina says. "We're about to go in right now. I need you. I need you to get here as fast as you can."

"I am…I'm coming right now," I say.

"Just pray, Kevin," Amina says. "We have to pray."

"I'm ten minutes away. Stay with my daughter!" I scream.

* * * *

Another call is coming in. Shit.

"Yeah," I say into the phone without checking the caller ID.

"So you finally answer the phone," Lisa says.

"I don't have time for your sarcasm, Lisa. I'm on my way to the hospital. If you called to pick a fight, now is not the time."

"Why are you going to the hospital?" Lisa asks. "What's wrong with you?"

"It's not me, Lisa. It's… it's… Aaliyah," I tell her. "Amina's taking her to Harlem Hospital."

"What happened, Kevin?"

"I don't know the details. But Aaliyah's been shot," I tell her, scarcely understanding the words coming out of my mouth.

"What the fuck do you mean our daughter's been shot?" Lisa screams.

"I don't know anything," I say. "I have to go."

"Well, I'm going to the hospital too," Lisa says. "I want some fucking answers."

"Right. See you there," I say as I hang up the phone.

Lisa

Once I thought I wanted to be an actress so I got an acting coach. All the lessons I learned from him will be put to the test today. I have to give the performance of my life.

Kevin actually answered the phone and actually talked to

me. This couldn't be more perfect than if I wrote the script myself. The window has opened a crack, just enough for me to squeeze through and take back my man.

I rush in through the Emergency doors. Kevin and Amina are pacing the waiting area. I'm operating on sheer instinct and say the first thing that comes to mind.

"Bitch! What the fuck did you do to my daughter?" I scream as I run up to Amina and sock her in the jaw.

Amina hits me back and we start rocking. She gets in some good shots. I get in some good shots. But the fight doesn't last nearly long enough. Kevin pulls us apart before things get totally out of hand.

"This shit right here is not helping Aaliyah!" Kevin yells.

"I demand to know why this bitch put my daughter in jeopardy!" I scream. "Say whatever you want about things I didn't do. But one thing I never did was put that child in harm's way."

"I don't have to answer to you, Lisa!" Amina fires back. "There was nothing I could do! How could I expect some crazy person to start shooting a gun in the middle of the day in the middle of the street?"

"Bitch, this is fucking New York City!" I remind her. "And we're in Harlem. Shit ain't sweet around here. Maybe if you didn't have my daughter in the middle of the street then nothing would have happened to her in the middle of the street!"

"I didn't have her in the middle of the street," Amina says. "She jumped out of the taxi before I could stop her. It happened so fast. Somebody shot her that quickly. It was like they were intentionally gunning for us."

"Bitch, why the fuck would somebody want to shoot a little girl?" I scream. "Stop making fucking excuses. You fucked up! I swear you'd better pray that my daughter is OK because I'm gonna beat the tar off of your ass. And Kevin ain't gonna be able to pull me off you next time!"

"I told you that this is not getting us anywhere," Kevin says.

"I agree," Amina adds. "We all need to pull together to help Aaliyah. Right now she needs our prayers and support."

"She needed you not to be so damned irresponsible and maybe none of us would be here right now," I reply sarcastically.

"You know what?" Kevin says to Amina. "Why don't you go back to the house? I can't deal with this friction right now. It's stressing me out. That's all it's doing."

"You want me to leave?" Amina asks. "Why don't you ask her to leave?"

"Amina, please, just do this for me," Kevin says. "I'll fill you in later."

"OK. If that's what you want," Amina says sadly, dropping her head as she shuffles away.

I'm smiling inside and no one can even tell. This isn't the way I planned for things to unfold. All I really wanted was to take Amina out of the equation. But by shooting Aaliyah, I have a different avenue to get back with Kevin *and* destroy Amina. That's even better. Things are working out better than I could have hoped.

Kevin

How could Amina have put my child at risk? I would never have imagined anything like this happening, especially not with Amina. She seemed so on point all the time. Aaliyah was in the middle of the street? What bullshit was that?

Lisa's a bad role model, a horrible cook and she doesn't try to be a friend to Aaliyah. But she's right. I have to agree with her. No one ever physically harmed Aaliyah when she was in Lisa's care.

My world is spinning.

Sensing my pain, Lisa lays a hand on my arm and tries to console me. I didn't realize she could be compassionate.

****

"Sir," the surgeon says as he walks over to me. His face mask is pulled down under his chin and his eyes look exhausted. He's got me worried.

"My daughter? How is she?" I ask in desperation.

"We did everything we could for her. She lost a lot of blood. We couldn't keep up with the bleeding. I'm sorry to have to tell you this but your daughter didn't make it. She expired at five-thirteen."

I'm in shock. Just like that, my daughter is dead. Aaliyah

is gone. What am I going to do now?

****

"I am not turning my back on you, Amina. I'm just very angry right now. I need to be alone for a while until I get my head on straight," I say. "Take the money and go stay in one of those nice hotels in Manhattan."

"What? I don't want money, Kevin!" Amina says. "I want to be with you. We should be together."

"I can't right now. I just can't be with you," I reply. "You know that I've been honest with you. I blame you for not doing more to protect my daughter and now she's dead. I can't see you for a while."

"How can you say that?" Amina asks.

"You didn't do your job, Amina! You promised to take care of my daughter and now she's dead — under your care. Aaliyah's dead!" I can't stand hearing the words coming out of my mouth. I break down. Amina tries to comfort me but I pull away.

"Kevin, we can get past this. If we ever needed each other before…" Amina starts but sees that I am not listening. "OK. I will respect your wishes. You want me to go, so I'll go. The second you need me, call me. Better yet, I'll check in on you."

"Don't," Kevin says. "Don't call me. Stay at the Marriott. Use the money I gave you. I'll call you when I'm ready. I'll call you."

Amina looks beaten and defeated but I can't worry about her. I have to figure out for myself how I'm going to make it through the next minutes, days, weeks.

CHAPTER TWENTY-TWO

Sleeping With the Enemy

Lisa

It's time to pack up and go home. I'm almost finished filling up my suitcase. A few more things, and I'm out. Staying at Malik's was convenient but now I have to go take care of my man.

Kevin's been calling me every day since Aaliyah died. He wants to reminisce about how wonderful and beautiful she was. He's hurting and he needs me.

It's funny how life works out. Aaliyah's death has turned out to be the best thing that could have happened for us. She was always getting in the way all the time anyway, whining and complaining. Truthfully speaking, and I'm not a coldhearted person, but I'm glad she's gone.

I stopped taking my birth control pills. Kevin always used to talk about having a baby with me so Aaliyah would have someone to play with. Back then, I wasn't ready to have no babies. Fuck that! I wasn't messing up this bomb ass body!

But that was then and this is now. Now I will do whatever I have to do to strengthen my position. I'll act as supportive as I possibly can but sooner or later, I'll have Kevin's ass back in bed, screaming my name. Once I finish working my magic on him, Amina will be permanently out.

****

"What's all this?" Malik asks when he sees my suitcase.

Shit, I wasn't expecting him to come back so early.

"Sorry, boo, but Kevin needs me to help him out for a little while," I say. "Don't give me that look. His daughter just died. What am I supposed to do when he calls me up crying on the phone?"

"Oh, I see. Now that he needs you, you go running. What about his new fiancée?" Malik asks. "Why can't she take care of him?"

"Please, Malik. Chill," I reply. "You're making something out of nothing. As soon as Kevin's sanity returns and he gets back on his feet, I'll be right back here. You don't have to worry about a thing."

I give Malik a quick peck on his lips and get the fuck out of Dodge.

I know that Malik thinks I'm a lying, scheming ass bitch, but I don't care. I'm doing what I have to do for myself.

I mean, come on! I always told him that even though he was cute as hell, I couldn't put my heart into him because of his lifestyle.

When the fuck did anything change to make him think things would be poppin' off between us?

Malik

Something's not right about this whole shit.

Lisa must think I'm an idiot. Does she really believe that I wouldn't put two and two together? *Malik, get me a heater.* She was so hot for that fucking gun.

And what did I do? I got her the fucking gun. And why? Because I love that ass of hers to pieces.

Maybe I am an idiot. But I know how to square this shit up.

Lisa

I don't knock when I get to the house. I just use the set of keys that I never returned.

When I walk in, I see Amina standing in the middle of the living room with tears in her eyes.

"Kevin? Why did you ask me to come help you if she's going to be here?" I ask. "You always said that she does a fine job taking care of you. If you have her, you don't need me."

"Actually," Kevin says. "Amina was just about to leave. We've put our engagement on hold."

"Well, don't let me stop you," I say as I open the door and step aside.

"I know that this isn't really what you want, Kevin, and the person you've been lately really isn't you," Amina says. "But if you really want to put us on pause, take back the ring."

Amina takes the engagement ring off her finger and hands it to him.

"That's not necessary," Kevin says. "I want you to keep it."

"I don't want to wear it if it has no meaning," Amina says. "If it ever does again, then you can ask me to marry you again"

Don't worry, bitch, I think. *I'll be rocking that ring as soon as you get your African ass out of here.*

I turn to Kevin and approach him affectionately as soon as the door closes. I plan to give him all the tender loving care he needs yet I don't want to be obvious. I reach into the closet, grab a set of sheets and throw them on the couch.

"What are you doing?" Kevin asks.

"I'm here for you," I say, "but at the same time I know you need your space. I'll sleep here. Call down if you need me."

"Actually, I need you to hold me tonight," Kevin says. "I may even need to cry on your shoulder."

"OK. But just don't think I'm trying to take advantage of the situation," I say. "I'm here for you because I'm your friend. I also respect the fact that you're not in love with me anymore. I don't want you to feel uncomfortable."

"I called and asked you to come here," Kevin says. "So if you don't mind, I'd like you to sleep in bed with me."

"Enough said," I reply.

I grab my suitcase and head towards the stairs. It's taking everything inside of me to not bust out laughing. I'm such a fucking actress.

Kevin

Sleeping with Lisa makes me feel better. We've been together for so long. She remembers when Aaliyah was just a baby. Back in the early days of our relationship when we were so happy being a little family.

I've asked her to clean out Aaliyah's room, pack all her clothes and give them to charity. I can't do it. It's too painful. Lisa agreed that she would have everything gone by the time I get back from work.

She just hugged me goodbye and told me not to worry. I like this side of Lisa. I feel now that I made a mistake in pushing her away, giving up so easily when I should have seen her side of things.

Work is what will help get me through. If I involve myself in other things besides grieving and reliving happier days, I think I'll be OK. God, I hope so. I need something to fill up the holes in my heart.

I've just turned the corner at then end of my street and a car pulls up next to me at the light. A black Benz. Nice car.

The passenger window slides down and I recognize the guy sitting behind the wheel.

"Yo," he calls out to me. "Remember me?"

"Yeah. You're Lisa's friend, right?"

He laughs. "I guess you could say we're a little more than friends. But yeah, you're right. Mind if I talk to you a minute?"

"Hey, Lisa is free to make up her own mind about…" I begin but a blast of car horns behind us drown me out. "Sure," I yell back at him. "Pull up over there."

We drive another half block and pull to the curb. I get out of my car, wondering what he could possibly have to say to me.

"Malik," he says by way of introduction and sticks out his hand. "We're both fucking the same bitch."

"That's one hell of a way to start a conversation," I say.

"The only way. It's what we got in common right now," he says.

"How did you know where to find me?" I ask.

"All Lisa ever does is complain about that hair braiding salon you got and about all those African bitches you got working for you. It wasn't hard to find the spot then follow you home," Malik tells me.

"OK. Tell me why you want to talk to me. And what did you mean when you said 'right now'? Lisa can do whatever she wants and…"

"I'm not here to make trouble for you and Lisa, Kevin," he interrupts me. "I'm here to rescue your ass from a world of hurt."

"Go on," I say, suspicious of his motivations but interested in what he has to say.

"About two months ago…," he begins.

At the end of his story, I feel like I'm going to throw up. And then I do.

Lisa

Malik has been blowing up my phone all afternoon. I decide to answer it for no other reason than to tell him to fall back.

"Malik, what is it?" I ask. "What the hell is so important for you to be calling me every ten minutes? You know I got shit to do."

"No. What I know is that you killed your boy's daughter," Malik says. "I know you fired the gun because there were fifteen shots in it when I gave it to you and now there's only ten. Five bullets are missing. You probably tried to kill the African chick and shot the little girl instead."

"Malik, you don't know what you're talking about," I say calmly. Inside, though, I'm dying. "You're talking nonsense right now."

"If I'm talking so much nonsense why don't I just have this discussion with the district attorney instead of you?" Malik asks.

"What do you want, Malik?" I ask.

"I want to know why you had to play me with your lies and shit," Malik says. "I mean, things were cool with us. Things always were good with us. You ain't have to try to make me think you were all into to me. I could have just kept knocking your back in. I would have been happy with that. I would have been happy just with that."

"Malik, don't act like that," I say. "Don't even talk like that. You know good and damn well that it was never just about sex with me. You wanted to lock me down, nigga."

"I'm a man like any other man," Malik says. "If I couldn't have you as my girl, I was content with getting the pussy."

"It's like that?" I ask.

"You made it like that," Malik says. "You're the one that tried to play me out, remember?"

"I keep trying to tell you that nobody tried to play you out," I reply.

"If you ain't trying to play me out, why the fuck are you there with that nigga and I'm here all by myself?" Malik asks.

"Malik, if you want me to come over, why don't you just ask me?" I say. "What's the point of getting into all of this other shit? You know the only reason I'm here is to console Kevin. His daughter died."

"Yeah, the only reason you're there is you feel guilty about killing his fucking daughter," Kevin says. "How 'bout that?"

"You know what? I'm on my way!" I say and hang up before Malik can respond.

So, he wants to play that way? That nigga don't even know who he's fucking with.

I throw on some sexy lingerie then a jacket over it. I'll seduce Malik alright. He's such an easy target, it won't be hard at all.

****

I tiptoe up the stairs and go straight to his bedroom.

"Is this what you wanted?" I ask as I drop the jacket on the floor. "All you had to do was ask and stop acting like a big ass fucking baby."

"Whatever," Malik says. "Bring your ass over here."

"No. You come and get it, nigga," I reply.

Malik slides across the bed and grabs at me. He starts kissing hungrily on my neck then on the cleavage that's popping out of my bra.

As he's nibbling on my neck, I see that he found the gun. It's sitting in plain sight on the dresser. Shit. He wasn't ever supposed to find it.

"What you so interested in, Lisa?" His eyes follow the same line as mine. "Oh, the gun. Clever bitch, hiding it behind the radiator. What, you're the only one watching cops and robbers on TV?"

"What are you blathering about?" I ask when I push him away.

"You think I didn't notice how you handled the heater. Never touching it with your fingers," he says.

"So what?" I pull at his belt and pull him closer to me as I kneel down at his feet. I pull down his pants then pull his dick out and start jerking it. I act like I'm about to put it in my mouth but then I pause.

"You weren't trying to think about setting me up for icing that little girl, were you?" he asks me.

"What the fuck you talking about? Why don't you just shut the fuck up and pull your goddamned shirt over that stupid head of yours," I say. He's got me cold and I'm about to panic.

Malik grabs the bottom of his shirt and pulls it over his head. I reach for the gun. It's in my hands and I flip off the safety. Bam!

Nothing happens.

I pull the trigger again and nothing happens. I keep squeezing off rounds and he doesn't go down.

"Shit, Lisa. I was hoping you wasn't gonna do that," Malik says as he tucks in his dick.

"And I was."

I hear a familiar voice behind me. It can't be! I lunge at Malik.

"You fuck! You piece of shit! You set me up!" I screech.

A strong set of hands grabs me from behind and pulls me off Malik.

"You know what Malik here said? He said the only thing we had in common was that we were both fucking the same bitch," Kevin whispers in my ear.

"So the fuck what? I told you I was fucking him!" I scream.

"Well, now we have another thing in common. You were trying to kill him just like you tried to kill Amina."

"I wanted that bitch dead! She stole you from me! Her and that fat African ass! Your daughter got in the way! That was a fucking accident. I never wanted to hurt Aaliyah," I explain as I struggle out of Kevin's arms.

"There you go, blaming a little girl for what you did," Malik says as he tugs his shirt back over his head.

"Why would you do this to me, Malik? I told you that we would never be a couple. I told you that…"

"Save it, Lisa," Malik says. "You didn't want to get with me because of my lifestyle. I got that. But you were trying to kill me. I didn't believe you'd try some shit like that. But Kevin said let's test you out. And sure as shit, you failed."

"Kevin! You didn't just believe him? Don't go telling me you believed his black ass!" I shout.

"Malik had no reason to lie to me. He could have shot me and then he would have had you all to himself," Kevin says. "But however much you don't like his lifestyle, he's no baby killer like you."

Kevin pushes me across the room and I land on the bed.

A second later, a trench coat and uniform fall into the room.

"Thank you, gentlemen," trench coat says. "I believe we've heard enough. Cuff her, Officer."

CHAPTER TWENTY-THREE

Lost in Harlem

Amina

Last night I checked into a cheap motel. Kevin gave me two thousand dollars to stay at a better place but if we are truly finished, I have to conserve what little money I have. How long will the money even last? Salima is right, I know nothing. I am naïve, just like she said.

So here I am in the middle of Harlem with next to nothing. I feel like crying again. But I have to remember that I do know at least one other person. She wouldn't help me then but maybe she'll help me now.

****

I'm waiting outside the hair braiding salon when Salima arrives.

"What are you doing here?" she asks me.

"Hello Salima," I say then I burst out crying.

"What happened now?" she asks me.

"Oh Salima! Kevin broke off our engagement," I cry.

Salima ushers me in and takes my bags from me. "Why don't you sit down," she tells me. I can see that she is already thinking about me asking her to stay with her and I get the feeling she's coming up with more excuses why I can't.

"Thanks," I say when she hands me a cup of water.

"I don't know what to say, Amina. Kevin's going through a tough time right now," she starts.

"So he asks me to leave? That does not make any sense. Now is when he needs me the most!" I start crying again.

"Girl, get a grip!" Salima orders. "You think just because he asked to be alone for a while means he doesn't care about you?"

"He can't. And with Lisa moving back in as I was walking out the door tells me that it really is over," I inform her.

"Lisa? Damn that girl works fast," Salima says almost with a touch of admiration.

"You can't be on her side!" I wail. "You don't even like her! And you're my only friend here in New York!"

A fresh round of tears come flooding out of my eyes. Can it really be that no one cares about me?

Salima hands me a box of tissues. "Amina, you really don't get how the game is played."

"If this is a game, then I don't want to play! Kevin is not the only one who lost Aaliyah. I did, too."

"The game I'm talking about is Lisa's game," she explains. "That bitch will do anything to keep Kevin. She's evil and Kevin is stupid enough to fall for her games. She pretends to love him. But she doesn't. She just doesn't want anyone else to have him. She wants to wrap him tight around her finger because she's a greedy bitch!"

I slump in my chair, half the box of tissues already gone. "What do I do now?" I ask her.

"You do what you have to," Salima says very matter of factly.

"And what does that mean?"

Salima sits next to me and explains, "You get a job. You find a room. You find a man. And you stay the hell away from this salon and Kevin."

"But Salima! How can I do all those things? You're my only friend!"

Salima seems to think this over. "What can you do, Amina?"

I am puzzled by her question. "Besides cook and clean?"

"Well, that's a start," she tells me. "I have a friend from back home who owns a small restaurant uptown. Maybe she can help you."

"I would appreciate whatever help you can give me. But I don't understand why I have to stay away from you."

Salima exhales heavily. "Amina, Kevin comes around here often. I never know when he's going to show up. You need to make him miss you and search high and low for you. Do you think this thing with Lisa is going to last? She'll be back to her lazy ass ways in no time and then he'll want you even more. Do I have to teach you everything?"

Salima is right. I have to forget Kevin for now. So I accept her friend's phone number and call her from the hotel room that afternoon.

****

I meet Lorraine, Salima's friend. Her restaurant, Taste of Africa, is small but business is good. She gives me a job as bus girl and within a week, I'm earning my own money for the first time in my life.

After a month, she tries me out in her kitchen. At first I just prepare the ingredients for the chef to throw together. I spend my mornings peeling and chopping vegetables. But before long, Lorraine is so impressed with my speed and efficiency, she asks me to do the shopping for the ingredients. Then she puts me in charge of making the sauces and condiments. Turns out I have a real flair for cooking.

And the best part is, I have been steadily getting raises. I am almost able to pay for an apartment of my own. And good thing, too. I have almost run out of Kevin's money.

****

I have been working at the restaurant for almost three months. Not a day goes by when I don't think of Kevin.

Every once in a while, I think I see him. But it is only my imagination. I imagine, also, that Lisa has made herself very comfortable again in Kevin's house. I pains me to believe that. I wanted to believe that Kevin is a better man than that.

It's Saturday morning and I have just finished shopping at the African market. It's still early and I decide to risk seeing Kevin and pop in on Salima.

Salima is surprised to see me. "Amina! Wow. What brings you here?" she asks me.

"I was in the neighborhood," I explain. "And I thought it would be nice to surprise you. Why? Aren't you surprised?" I ask with a smile.

"Um, well, sure I am. But you're taking a big chance. What if Kevin shows up?" she asks.

"I doubt that he will. It's is day off and it's early," I respond.

Just then, the door opens. I hear the tinkling of the little bell over the door. When I turn around, I gasp. Then I faint straight away.

****

When I come to, I remember this crazy dream. My eyes flutter open. Something smells really bad. I cough.

"Stop it! What is that horrible smell?'

"Oh, thank goodness you're awake! Amina, are you OK?" It's Salima.

"Yes, I think so," I tell her.

"I shoved some smelling salts under your nose. You fainted," she tells me.

I lift myself to my elbows and open my eyes. I almost faint again when I see who is next to Salima.

"Alou?"

He's the same man I knew back in Africa. The same man I married.

"Yes, Amina. It's me," he answers.

"You two know each other?" Salima asks.

I struggle up to my feet and wrap my arms around him. The warmth of his body has not cooled. The strength of his arms around me has not changed. "Yes," I tell her. "This is my Alou."

"Aaron?' Salima asks.

"No, his name is Alou," I practically scream. "He is who I have been looking for all this time! He is my husband!"

****

Alou gently unwraps my arms from around his waist and leads me to a chair. I cannot believe I am once again looking into his eyes.

"I thought you abandoned me," I say tearfully.

"And I thought the same of you," he says as he lifts up my chin so I can gaze into his deep brown eyes.

"Where were you? Where did they take you? Where have you been? I thought you had been deported. Everyone told me to forget about you!" I am so happy yet so full of questions that need to be answered.

I see Alou glance over at Salima. She thinks I am crazy.

"Amina, this is Aaron. He delivers supplies to the shop. Why do you keep calling him Alou?"

"Because he is my Alou!"

"It's true, Salima," Alou admits. "You know me as Aaron. I changed my name after I was arrested for stealing a car at JFK."

"You stole a car?" Salima asks.

"No, I didn't," Alou tells her. "I had borrowed my uncle's car to pick up Amina. It was all a big mistake," he explains.

"It better be. I don't want to be associating with no thief!" Salima declares.

"Stop it, Salima," I say. "I want to be happy right now. We have found each other. I am so happy!"

Again the two of them glance at each other.

"Well, congratulations," Salima says. "Now will you please go have this happy reunion somewhere else. I have a business to run!"

****

I almost forget my groceries. But at the last second I rush back into the shop to get them.

"I have to get to work!" I cry. What an awful thing to have to say to my true love.

"You have a job? I am so happy for you," Alou says.

"After I thought I lost you and everyone told me to forget you, I had to do something. A friend abandoned me for his former fiancée and I was utterly alone." My story pours out of me. "And now that I have found you, we can get married here in America as we planned and have a bunch of children! I cannot wait to call my father and tell him the good news."

Alou hugs my shoulder and pulls me close. It feels exactly the same as I remember. Nothing has changed between us.

"Where are you living?" he asks me.

"At a ratty hotel on the west side of Harlem. Where do you live?"

"I live with roommates over on East 119th Street," he tells me.

"Well, I'd love to meet them! When can we be together?" I am so excited to begin the life I dreamed of almost a year ago. I can hardly believe my good luck. Allah has been watching over me all along.

"As soon as possible," Alou says. "I think we should make our marriage official as soon as possible."

"Oh, Alou!" I croon. "I am so happy you still feel the same way about me. I really thought we were lost to each other. Now our lives will be perfect!"

"Yes they will, Amina. Yes they will."

CHAPTER TWENTY-FOUR

Hard Truths

Kevin

I've been scouring the city, looking for Amina. For the umpteenth time, I plan to harass Salima. Up until now, she hasn't told me shit. But I know she's spoken to Amina. Who else in the city does Amina know?

"Kevin. Not you again," Salima says distastefully when I walk into the salon. "Why don't you go somewhere else? You kicked my girl out of your house and moved that psycho bitch back in. And you did it after she killed your little girl."

"Salima," I say, trying not to lose my cool. "Lisa is in jail. She's paying for her crimes. OK? She is no longer a part of my life. How many times do I have to repeat myself? It's been months."

"Tell it to someone who cares, Kevin," she says. "I don't give a shit about you and your business."

"Oh, really?" I say. Suddenly Salima is interested. "Let's go in the back room and discuss it."

We move the conversation into the privacy of the back room.

"I know what goes on in here," I tell Salima.

"And what would that be?" she replies.

"Just try to pretend you don't know. I've been looking the other way because I didn't want to be implicated in your illegal activities. I could very convincingly claim ignorance," I tell her.

"And? You going to get to the point or not?" she asks me.

"As crazy as Lisa is, she told me some very interesting things. And you know her. She always had an ear to the streets," I drag it out. "I know you run illegal prostitution back here. After hours when everyone thinks the salon is closed."

"Don't try to bullshit me!" she spits out. "You don't know shit!

"Aaron," I say and her face turns pale.

"Who's that? I never heard of him," she lies.

"Don't give me that bullshit. You know exactly who I'm talking about."

"Lisa told you this?" Salima asks nervously. "Who's going to believe her?"

"It doesn't matter if the cops believe her or not. What matters is whether or not I plant a little seed," I tell her.

"You're crazy, Kevin! You'd risk this salon to destroy

me?"

I have never seen Salima this anxious before. She's trying to cover it up but I got her number.

"I would destroy everything I own if I can't have
Amina," I say matter of factly.

Salima glares at me. I can see that she is debating
whether or not to call my bluff.

"The past is the past," I say. "What happened has already happened. I can't take it back. But I can make it up to
Amina by making her the happiest woman in the world. I
want to marry her. You are going to help me find her or so
help me, your entire world will come crashing down around
you."

"You're too late, Kevin," Salima finally says. "She already has someone else."

"Who is he?" I demand.

"Kevin, give it up. That is my only advice to you," Salima tells me.

"You know what, Salima, I'm not playing with your ass
anymore!" I say sternly. "Tell me what I need to know or
I'll call the cops!"

"You can't be serious," Salima says.

"I know what you don't want me to know, Salima. Not
only about the illegal prostitution you've got going on here.
I also know you've been stealing from me. I know that
you've lied about me. I know that you took money — my
money — from Lisa and supplied her with information so
she could spy on me. I know you contributed to my daugh-

ter's death!"

"How can you know all this? Did that murderous bitch tell you?" Salima asks nervously.

"As a matter of fact, she did. She tried to deal down her sentence by providing information on you and other individuals. But she was declared incompetent and delusional. The courts think she's insane. And you know what? She is. But that doesn't mean I don't believe her.

"Salima, I don't give a fuck about the salon if I can't have Amina," I snap.

"You're serious," she says.

"As a heart attack," I reply.

I follow Salima to the receptionist's desk. She rips a sheet of paper off a pad and jots something down. "This is where she's at," Salima says. "Good luck."

I ignore Salima and rush out the door. When I get in the car, I'm mortified by what I read.

This can't be fucking happening.

Amina

As I look at the crowd gathered around me, I can't believe what is about to happen. I can't believe that this will be the fulfillment of all the dreams I had for coming to America in the first place.

I wonder what Kevin is doing and if he's thinking about me. He doubted me, after everything I did for him and his

203

daughter. To not believe in me, to not understand my pain over what happened, was too much for me to swallow. Yet I think about him every day.

Even since I found my Alou again.

I am so deeply lost in my thoughts, I can barely hear the singing. I can't hear the words being spoken. I can't decipher the meaning in anything.

Then with a little nudge from Alou, I snap out of it and am once again aware of my surroundings.

Alou. My African husband. Aaron, soon to be my American husband. I will soon be American, too.

My fairy tale ending is just moments away.

The justice of the peace turns to the small audience and asks, "Is there anyone present who has any reason to oppose this union between Amina and Aaron?" the preacher asks. "Speak now or forever hold their peace."

"Noooooooooooooooooooooooooooo!" a man's voice booms out.

I turn around and see Kevin running down the aisle.

"Amina! No! You can't marry him!" Kevin hollers.

"Stay where you are, young man!" the preacher orders. "Why do you object to this union?"

Kevin bends over at the waist with his hands on his knees as he catches his breath.

"This man's name is not Aaron," Kevin says.

"I have seen his birth certificate, sir. I can assure that his name is indeed Aaron."

"It's a lie!" Kevin says. "This man is a liar!"

"Kevin!" I yell. "What are you talking about?"

"This man convinces young African women to marry him and then he sells them into prostitution!"

"What? That is absurd, Kevin! I don't believe…"

At that exact moment, a half dozen police burst into the church.

"Arrest him!"

Alou jumps up onto the alter and scrambles over it. He is gone in a flash. Three police officers race down the aisle after him and the other three head back out the door to pursue him on the street.

Kevin runs over to me and scoops me in his arms, pulling me away from the mayhem.

Everything happens so fast. I look at Kevin as he guides me to a bench. In his eyes I see relief. And love.

"Would you mind explaining to me what is going on, Kevin?" I demand of him.

"Lisa saved us," I tell her.

"What?!" I exclaim. "She hates me. She would never help me. Why, you two are engaged again! Why would she save us?"

Kevin pulls me close and laughs. "Oh, honey! Don't you ever read the newspaper?"

"What has that got to do with anything? You better start explaining yourself!"

"I promise I will. As soon as we have that preacher marry us."

I stare at Kevin like he's gone insane. And then I melt

into his arms. I have missed him so much, more than I ever missed Alou if the truth be told. And I believe in him. And if I need any actions to back up his words, here I am, cradled in his arms again with him kissing my face in joy and relief.

Kevin has rescued me again. Kevin, my savior.

CHAPTER TWENTY-FIVE

Happy Ending

Amina

Kevin and I got married that very same day even though we had to wait for the police investigation to finish. It's been four months now, and I'm happy, the happiest I've ever been.

We haven't taken a honeymoon yet. But truthfully, every day is like a honeymoon. I know Kevin does not want me to leave the country until we're secure about my citizenship status.

And because I am three months pregnant.

We talk about our honeymoon. Kevin has suggested Brazil, the Dominican Republic and Jamaica. I keep telling him that I want to bring him to Africa and introduce him to my family. Kevin shoots the idea down every time. I think he's afraid.

I don't love Alou anymore. I have given my heart to

Kevin completely. But I think it did Kevin some good to be worried that he'd lose me to another man.

We don't mention her, but I have gotten over Lisa one hundred percent. In the end, she undermined herself in more ways than one and ruined her life in the process. I still feel sorry for her. But not that sorry.

Lorraine and I have been in negotiations for me to buy the restaurant. Kevin thinks it is a wonderful idea. I'm thinking I'd rather raise my family than be a working mother. Then I think it would be great to have someone cooking for me every night.

Salima was arrested. After Kevin told me what she had been doing at the salon — stealing from the till, shorting him on receipts, and engaging in prostitution — I understood a little bit better why she didn't want me coming around. Also, it turns out she knew Aaron was Alou from the beginning. She hid the information from me so she could continue her illegal activities without my intereference. She knew that I would have told Kevin everything.

I have not told my family anything about Alou. They would not believe me in any event. He had everyone convinced that he was a U.S. citizen and that he really loved me. I don't know what to believe and I will probably never learn the truth. Anyway, a small part of me wants the fairy tale to remain pure. But the larger part no longer cares.

I'm a woman married to a wonderful man, pregnant with her first child, and about to become a naturalized citizen.

What could be better? I can't wait to tell my parents!

CHAPTER TWENTY-FIVE

Letter to My Family

Amina

My Dearest Family,

I apologize for not writing sooner. So much has happened and I've held back because I did not want you to worry about me when I am so many miles away. Notice that I did not say miles away from home. A wise man (Dad) once told me that home is where the heart is and I have found a new home here in America.

My flight was fine. We even arrived ahead of schedule. My problems started when Alou did not come to get me. I waited for hours and hours.

Eventually, I realized that I would have to find him. I showed the return address ot the girl at Information and she told me how to take the New York City subway to the location.

After I got off the subway and set foot on the streets of New York for the very first time, a group of three men attacked me. Don't worry! Nothing bad happened to me. A man, a good samaritan, jumped out of his car and came to my rescue. He punched one of the men and chased them all away. Needless to say I was so thankful that Allah put this man in exactly the right place at exactly the right time.

Afterwards, he was kind enough to drive me to Alou's apartment building. When we arrived, the building was surrounded by I.N.S. agents. The man, Kevin, knew one of the agents from seeing him around the neighborhood and said that his presence was bad news for Alou, that he was conducting an investigation and Alou had most likely been deported.

I had very little money as you know and I knew no one except for my new friend, Kevin. He took pity on me and invited me to stay with him and his daughter in his house in Harlem.

I slept on his couch while I figured what to do. His fiancée, Lisa, put me to work taking care of the house to pay my room and board, and I became his daughter's guardian as well. But tragedy struck and the daughter, a beautiful little girl named Aaliyah, fell victim to random violence which turned out not to be random at all.

Lisa had become jealous of me and tried to remove me from the picture. Aaliyah's death was accidental but Kevin blamed me for not protecting her properly. Our friendship came to an abrupt end after a few short months.

As it turned out, Lisa was responsible for Aaliyah's death and is now in jail awaiting trial. Feeling miserable that he falsely accused me of being negligent, Kevin resumed our friendship.

To be honest, I had my reservations. But then I thought about how kind he had been to take me into his home and to give me shelter. Understandably, he needed time to heal after his daughter's death and come to terms with what his fiancée had done.

I was miserable without Alou but I had to come to terms with it. By now, you have probably heard from his family and know what has become of him. I do not.

In any event, Kevin and I fell in love and four months ago, in the American tradition, we properly consummated our relationship by getting married! Yes, I am now Mrs. Kevin Wright.

Kevin is the sweetest, kindest man in the world. He raised his daughter on his own after his wife died during childbirth. He is a successful businessman and a good provider. I promise you that is not an over-statement. He employs women from the Motherland at the hair braiding salon he owns. He also owns two apartment buildings. He has been a godsend to me and I'm lucky to have met him.

More than anything, I want all of you to share in

my joy. I want all of you to share in my promise. You don't have to worry about my being deported because I now am an American citizen! Your dream for me has come true.

All Kevin wants is for me to be happy. He has enrolled me in school and soon I will be pursuing a degree in Education. He provides me with clothing, food, jewelry, and an allowance. I have a gorgeous engagement ring and diamond wedding band. And most importantly, I am safe and secure under his roof on a beautiful tree-lined street in Harlem.

In closing, I am so, so happy and I pray that you are all just as happy for me. I made it through the storm thanks to Allah, and Allah was benevolent enough to send me Kevin.

Your loving daughter, sister, niece, and cousin,

Amina

CHAPTER TWENTY-SIX

Letter from the Elders

Amina

A few weeks later, much sooner than I expected, the mail-man catches me just as I am about to go back inside after sweeping the steps. He hands me a letter with foreign postage affixed to it. I rush inside and open the envelope in the living room. I sit on the couch to read it.

Dear Amina,

We, the Elders of your tribe, recently received some very disturbing news. From your family we have learned that you have married an American man without their blessing.

This man was not born and raised under the same tenets, morals and culture as you were and will not be able to contribute to the perpetuation of our society in America. In essence, you will forget what we have taught you because you will no longer be living as one of us.

Needless to say, not only have you disappointed your fellow tribespeople, you have shocked and outraged your family who consider your actions rash and irresponsible.

Your family has taken a very firm stance that we elders support. You are to remove this man from your life and concentrate on a future with Alou. If you do not, your family will disown you and no longer consider you their daughter.

Our opinion of African American men is that they are deplorable. They are lazy and lack culture. They spend too much time trying to kill each other. They waste their time not doing much except finding ways to scheme off the government and/or anyone they can. They poison their bodies, dress like gangsters, and are disrespectful. We cannot imagine why you would want to lose yourself to a man who is so very far beneath you in every way.

Amina, you are a smart young woman. We agreed to send you to America so you could build a better life there with Alou than the two of you could have had here. Your value to your family, and to your tribe, as Alou's American wife will increase over time.

Have you forgotten that you and Alou were married in accordance with the laws of our tribe? We will not recognize your American marriage. We do not care what the monster you now call husband gives you materialistically. Alou, and only Alou, is the man for you.

Alou has returned to the Motherland and has advised us of your situation. He will remain here and wait for your return, which we expect within the next year.

In the meantime, break off your relationship with the African American, get your citizenship on your own merit, and restore your faith in the path we have chosen for you.

We understand that you were at a disadvantage when you met this man. We fear that he has conned you by casting a spell over you. We fear you are using drugs and alcohol. Alou alluded to some very nasty goings on in his household that you confirmed when you revealed that a young girl had been murdered. We do not want you to live in such an environment. Your family did not spend all its money sending you to America so you could live in such an environment. And we most definitely do not believe you will thrive in such an environment.

We will not tolerate your betrayal of your family and culture. It is painful for us to repeat our decision, but if you continue with this nonsense, you will be dead to your family and the entire village. You will not become demonized by this American. Let this evil man worship the devil on his own. Allah has already claimed you to be his loyal servant. Now it is up to you to show us that you can truly remain loyal. We are counting on you. We hope you don't disappoint us.

The Council of Elders

I am crying by the time I finish the letter. I have never been so disturbed before. I must believe the Council of Elders is serious but I don't want to.

Kevin and I are going out later and I want to look my best. Crying right now is not a good idea. I think I'll just lay down and close my eyes for a while.

As I drift off to sleep, one word lingers in my mind and I am asleep before I can understand why.

Alou.

CHAPTER TWENTY-SEVEN

First Hearing

Lisa

I was all set to regain my place in Kevin's life and now look where I am. I have my first hearing this afternoon and my lawyer says I should start talking.

I'm in my cell, deep in thought, when the C.O. raps on the bars and tells me that I have a visitor. I wonder who it is. My sister has disowned me and I don't have any friends to speak of. Maybe it's Kevin!

To my surprise, when I sit down in front of the Plexiglas window, bitch-ass Malik is on the other side. I can't believe he'd come to talk after his betrayal. I pick up the phone.

"What up, Shorty?"

"Don't fucking 'what up Shorty' me!" I reply angrily as my eyes shoot daggers at him. "You fucking snitching and making shit up is what's up! Now you tell me what's up with that?"

"I don't know what you're talking about," Malik replies.

"Nigga, don't try to play me!" I snap.

Malik throws his hands in the air and shrugs his shoulders as if to say he doesn't know what I'm talking about.

"How could you do it to me, Malik?" I ask. "The cops weren't checking for me and they didn't know shit about you. Now you gave them a place to start when they had none and just enough incentive to start digging into shit they had no clue about. Are you that stupid that you didn't think they'd check you out? Come to think of it, why isn't your ass locked up already? You're here because you're worried about what I'm gonna do. You got yourself jammed up, didn't you? I'm walking out that door. But you on the other hand are never gonna see the light of day again once they...."

"Lisa," Malik says calmy. "Keep your mouth shut. You're on some bullshit. They ain't coming at me and they ain't got shit on you. All you've gotta do is keep your mouth shut. That's why I came here."

"To tell me to keep my mouth shut?" I repeat. "All *I* gotta do? Nigga, all *you* had to do was keep *your* motherfucking mouth shut. Don't forget that you're the one who put me in here."

"No, you put yourself in here," Malik says, sounding just like a bitch. "You were trying to play *me* out, remember? You were trying to set me the fuck up."

"Hello? How the fuck was I setting you up when nobody knew nothing about nothing?" I ask. "You're the one who gave the cops the lights to turn on. It's not my fault that all the lights are gonna shine on you now."

"Again, this is why I came here. Shut the fuck up. For real," Malik says. "All you gotta do is be quiet. I got a couple of dollars for you to get a real lawyer. And when you get out of here, just keep on keeping your mouth shut."

"We were both already in the clear until you did some bitch shit, Malik," I say angrily. "Ain't it obvious to you that the prosecutor only has circumstantial evidence against me? He has no evidence that I shot anybody! No eyewitnesses, no bullet casings…"

"And no gun," he interrupts.

"What?" I ask, stunned.

"That gun you fired at me was not the gun I gave you," he says with a sly smile on his face.

"So you didn't find it?"

"Oh I found it alright. You must think I'm fucking stupid, Lisa, if you think I didn't," he syays.

"Well, I, uh…,"

"Keep on acting like you don't know what I do and how much power I have," Malik whispers into the phone. "I have as many people having my back in here as I do on the streets."

"So you're threatening me, Malik?" I ask.

"Yeah, I am. And you wanna know why?" he asks in a way that sends chills up and down my spine.

"Why, Malik?"

"Because I'm gonna own your ass," he tells me.

I roll my eyes and turn to look for the guard. I'm about to put the phone down but he wags his finger, no.

"Oh, it's like that?" I ask.

"Yeah it's like that. You made it like that," he says angrily. "You're gonna lay your ass down in the bed you made for yourself."

****

I'm surprised to see Kevin in the courtroom. The way he's looking at me crushes me to my soul. I turn away.

I imagine how he's going to feel when some truths come out today. My truths, at any rate. I'll create a little reasonable doubt of my own.

I spin my tale. Malik was so jealous of my relationship with Kevin that he made up a story so Kevin would hate me. I apologize for being involved with two men at the same time. I explain how confused I was about the living situation I found myself in with my fiancé. I break down in tears when I talk about Aaliyah. I get indignant over the betrayal by both of the men in my life and their jumping to the conclusion that I was responsible for the death of a little girl I loved so much. Yada, yada. Again the actress in me resurfaces.

I lift my eyes to look at Kevin. I can't tell if my words have had any effect on him or not. But at least he was here and heard me. If he leaves the courtroom confused, I've succeeded.

Coming Soon...

Amina
Comes to Harlem
Part 2

By

Sidi

Amina arrives from West Africa happily anticipating a reunion with her tribal husband, Alou. She spots him just outside the terminal. His panicked eyes meet hers for a split second then he is shoved into the back seat of a police car. "Find me!" he screams as he is driven away.

Rescued by good samaritan, Kevin, Amina starts her new life in America learning lessons the hard way – namely from Kevin's jealous and conniving fiancée, Lisa. Lisa will stop at nothing to keep her man. So when Kevin's daughter is shot down in broad daylight, is Lisa responsible? Or is her sexy drug-dealing boyfriend Malik? Or was it all Amina's fault? Who will go to prison and who will be exonerated? And who will Kevin choose – Lisa or Amina? And then the final drama…what will Amina's family do when they learn she has broken from the plan the tribal Elders had programmed for her?

Amina Comes to Harlem Part 2 is a fast-paced story about the drama that goes down in Harlem every day. Learn the fate of all your favorite characters with each page filled with twists and turns that leave you wanting more!

Preview a new novel by

Sidi

Tamika

Part Two

The Saga of a Jamaican Girl Continues

A novel by

Sidi

PROLOGUE

"Mamacita, can you let me hear some more of that Rastafarian speak?" Jose asks.

Jose is the local Colombian who's been showing Tamika around and filling her in on every nuance of the country.

"Well, you know I'm tired of doing that, Jose," Tamika says. "And what did I tell you about calling me Mamacita? I told you that I'm a princess."

"Mamacita is just a sign of respect, my princess," Jose says.

"Not your princess, Jose," Tamika says. "Just Princess. I don't know you like that. Besides, not everybody who kin dem teet wit is fren."

"That's what I'm talking about, Princess," Jose says, laughing. "That sounds fabuloso. What the hell does it mean?"

Tamika smiles devilishly while playing with her gun inside her sweat jacket pocket.

Bang. Bang. Bang.

Tamika's lieutenant, Roger, who was handling Long Island for her, slumps down on the ground after being shot dead.

"It means that not everyone who smiles in your face and pretends to laugh with you is your friend," Tamika says. "Sometimes they are actually laughing at you because they are secretly your enemy and doing everything they can do in the dark to bring you down."

Tamika kicks Roger's dead body. "You see, you're a joke to them. That's why they show you their teeth. But you know about the law of the jungle, don't you Jose? If a lion shows you his teeth that means he's about to bite the shit out of you. That's why I'm always careful about people who call themselves my friend, smiling in my face. And while they think they're playing me, I'm always thinking of the way I'm going to play them."

"You's a cold one, Princess," Jose says.

"And that's why I'm still alive after all the shit I've been through," Tamika says. "I may be the coldest bitch in this entire world. But it's not like I don't have my reasons."

Tamika sighs, wondering if it was totally smart to kill Roger. Despite the fact that he's been hating on her for a while, and skimming profits, he wa a lieutenant in her organization and she's not sure how the other lieutenants will deal with how she handled him.

She has enough problems on her hands with so many people still believing that she killed her Colombian connection and lover, Ramos. She doesn't need any more drama.

"Well, such is life," Tamika says to herself before going about the business of ensuring she exports all the cocaine that she needs to send to New York City from Colombia.

With her Rastafarian dad and ex-head of the Unity of Jamaican Brothers (UOJB) dead, and with her taking over the reigns, it's her job to find the drug connections. But she plans to take things a step further. Tamika wants to be the connection.

"So, are you OK, Jose?" Tamika asks. "Are you ready to finish up or do you need a minute?"

"I'm always ready to make money, Princess," Jose says. "And if you pull this shit off that you are trying to do, I know I will never want for money."

"You've got that right," Tamika says. "No one in this entire country will want for money. Well, at least no one on our team. You can't take care of everybody."

"Yeah, fuck the bastards we don't know." Jose says. "They're bloodsuckers anyway."

"And I can't afford to have anyone sucking my blood," Tamika says. "I already have enough people eating off my plate."

Tamika looks up in the air towards her father Marley as she follows Jose, continuing their quest to ensure that she can supply everyone who's anyone in New York City with her drugs.

CHAPTER ONE

Marley & Tamika Return to NYC

Several months prior in Kingston, Jamaica.

"Tamika, Tamika, we have to come soon to town," Marley says to his daughter as he approaches her room in the place he's renting in Nine Miles, where Bob Marley was born. "The Tourism Board is putting on an event to prepare for the big Reggae festival in New York City next week."

"Hold on," Tamika whispers into her cell phone and hides it before her father reaches her room. "I wasn't even planning on going, Dad," Tamika says. "But if I have to go I'll find something to wear and get ready."

"Why you not ready, Tamika?" Marley asks. "This is very big deal. We have to get ready for the festival."

"I know, Dad," Tamika says. "That's why I'm resting and trying to mellow out. I know that man you can't beat you have fe call him fren like you said. I can't fight everybody when we get back to New York. I'm just trying to get my mind right."

Marley looks at his daughter suspiciously as if he's wondering why all of a sudden she's decided to listen to what he's been telling her all along.

"Well, you stay," Marley says. "I go to the planning session."

Marley backs out of the room still looking at Tamika suspiciously.

Tamika listens intently as her dad walks down the spiral staircase. When she hears the door open and close she knows it's safe. She picks up her phone and resumes her conversation.

"Haven't I been good to you, Carlo?" Tamika asks. "Haven't I helped you and a lot of people that are close to you eat?"

"Of course you have, Tamika," Carlo says. "What kind of a question is that?"

"I'm just saying that you should be down with me. That's all," Tamika says. "The Colombian cartels smuggled billions of dollars worth of cocaine into the United States. And it doesn't matter that they've bribed bankers, lawyers, judges, cops, and federal agents. We're the only ones with the money, power, respect, and discipline to move that type of product. We could be legendary, Carlo. Years from now when people start talking about they're telling the real story of how cocaine flooded Harlem, they'll be talking about us. We'll be the Dons. Our faces will be shown. Our stories will be told. And why shouldn't it be us? Why shouldn't we benefit from the discounted price that they're selling pure cocaine for? We have to jump on this now before the undisciplined crews fuck it up for everybody. And we can't have that. Can we?"

"So what do you want me to do kill all the rival gangs off?" Carlo asks.

"No. Not that," Tamika replies. "That would be like we're looking down on the people that are beneath us. And you should never look down on someone unless you're trying to pick them up. That's where we come in. We have to train any squad that's willing to work with us. But at the same time, we have to know that every man who kin dem teet wid u is not fren. We have to weed them out. If they smile in our faces but we hear that they're talking shit about us behind our backs we have to deal with them. Now, I know you've heard some things. I'm just asking you to deal with the people that you've heard shit about. Send a fucking message, Carlo. When bodies start falling left and right everybody will know that it's because the Princess of Harlem is on her way back. I don't want no shit when I get back there either. I want every stinking person that I cross paths with to feel thankful that they're still alive after I look upon their faces. I want you to make the shottas go clap, clap, Carlo. I want it to be no doubts that these streets are ours."

"What does Marley say about this?" Carlo asks.

"He is my dad and I love him dearly but we're not on

the same page right now," Tamika says. "He thinks that everyone should hold hands and sing a Bob Marley ballad in unison. Meanwhile, those that are behind us are gaining ground because they're hungrier than we are. You think that those type of people are gonna respect us because we're feeding other people? How can we ask them to not be grimy when they ain't eating off of our plates? A hungry man has to eat, Carlo. So, either we're going to feed them or we have to take them out if they don't want to sit at our table. That's all I'm asking you to do. Like Beanie Sigel said in the State Property movie. Niggas have to either get down or lay down. I expect for you to make that start happening before I get there."

"And what do I get out of it for doing that?" Carlo asks.

"I swear, Carlo, I mean no disrespect," Tamika says. "I love Roy. Him and my dad have been friends for years so he's like a grandfather to me. But he's taking forever to give you a stronger position in the organization. I'm not asking you to step on his toes or anybody's toes in the organiza- tion. I'm just saying that you deserve a leg up. That's what I can give you. You know that I have the money and power to make that happen. I can't do it by myself, though. You're the missing piece like Ramos used to be. So, let's join forces and make this happen."

"So, what's my percentage?" Carlo asks.

"Don't worry about that," Tamika says. "You know that you're gonna eat. With me, everybody eats."

"True," Carlo says. "Well, I guess I'll get to work then."

Without saying another word Tamika smiles and closes her cell phone. She feels content that she's back in the game.

****

Carlo grabs a bunch of his grimiest crew members and tells them to grab their heat and meet up with him in Brooklyn at a pool bar near 161st.

"There's no other way to say this than to just say it," Carlo says. "We have to take advantage of this money that's being left on the table. I haven't been eating enough lately and I'm more than hungry. So we're going to soften the streets up then partake of some of that good shit the Colombians just brought in here. Then maybe the hunger pains will go away."

"Not to go against what you're saying because I love to get play war games," says the power player called Hannibal since he's a beast like Hannibal Lector.

Hannibal is five feet nine inches tall with a bald head and massive shoulders. He has so muscular that people kid him all the time about not having a neck. Despite being able to break someone in half using his bare hands and two hundred eighty pound muscular frame, Hannibal fancies a Colt 45 revolver to do his dirty work for him when it's time.

"So, after we bust heads open how will we be able to afford to partake in that Colombian shit?" Hannibal asks.

"They're dealing in heavy weight only. We could all chip in everything that we have and still fall short."

"That's a good question, Hannibal," Carlo says. "But don't sweat it because we have help." The group looks at Carlo curiously. "The princess of Harlem is about to come back."

"Word? Tamika?" Hannibal asks.

"Yeah, Tamika," Carlo says. "And you know how she's living."

"Hell yeah," Hannibal says. "We get to wild the fuck out now."

Hannibal gives pounds and shakes hands with many of the other members of the crew.

"That's right," Carlo says. "Go out into the streets shooting first and asking questions later. If there's anybody that you feel suspect about just take his ass out. Take out his entire fucking crew if you have to. But if you think that a crew would benefit from our guidance and we would benefit from them, let those types of motherfuckers live. We have to get at this paper. And we have less than a week before Tamika gets here. Let's make her feel welcome. And let's make sure that she doesn't change her mind about backing us financially."

"Yeah, 'cause we need that," Hannibal says, thinking about the stories he heard about everyone in Tamika's previous squad being given a million dollar signing bonus for working with her.

****

Hannibal and Li'l Timmy sit in a Gypsy Cab on 111th St. in Harlem. They are spying on a shiesty dealer named Bingo due to his gambling habits.

"How long are you going to be?" asks the Driver.

"Chill the fuck out," Li'l Timmy barks. "I gave you a hundred dollars and we ain't been in your cab for five fucking minutes yet."

Li'l Timmy is a four feet six inches tall midget that yields an overwhelming napoleon complex. But in his instance, his bark is not bigger than his bite.

You will rarely ever spot Li'l Timmy without his Nine Millimeter pistol and steel coated, cop killer bullets. And everyone knows that with Li'l Timmy's temper it doesn't take much for him to whip out his gun and pull the trigger.

Li'l Timmy and Hannibal are stalking Bingo waiting for the best opportunity to ambush him. They are sitting in the cab with no masks.

"Why should we wear masks?" Hannibal asks when Li'l Timmy brings up the subject. "If somebody sees us and says to the Jakes that a big ass nigga and a midget did this who the fuck do you think that they're gonna pin it on knowing that we hang together so much? It's better for us to be straight gangsta with it and look everybody around us in their eyes after we do it. That's the best way to let motherfuckers know that they'd better keep their damned mouths shut."

"You's one straight gangsta ass nigga," Li'l Timmy says.

"Why, thank you very much," Hannibal replies. "You ain't so bad yourself."

* * * *

As Hannibal and Li'l Timmy watch Bingo a couple guys that he knows walks up to him. They pull out wads of money, wave them in the air, then throw a pair of dice against the wall.

Bingo starts laughing and reaches into his pocket pulling out his own wad of money. Then he picks up the dice, has a few words with the two guys and throws them into the wall.

A few words are spoken before all three men throw money on the ground. Bingo starts shaking the dice in his hand and throws them against the wall again. Obviously, he's trying to hit his number.

Hannibal taps Li'l Timmy on the shoulders and nods his head in the direction of Bingo. Then he opens the door and gets out the cab, waiting for Li'l Timmy to follow him.

"Don't go nowhere," Li'l Timmy says to the driver. "We'll be right back."

Li'l Timmy leaves the door open as they walk towards Bingo. He wants to be able to jump right back into the cab after he and his partner finishes putting in work.

"Times up, Bingo," Hannibal says when he walks up to Bingo from behind and smashes him across the face with his

45.

Bingo hollers in pain and the two thugs that are in the dice game with him jump back, leaning against the stoop.

"That's right," Li'l Timmy says. "You can kiss the motherfucking baby."

"What's this about?" Bingo asks.

"Your next in command can ask us that when you're gone," Hannibal says.

Buck. Buck. Buck. Buck. Buck.

Hannibal and Li'l Timmy shoot Bingo up in broad daylight before turning calmly and walking back to the cab.

Everyone that sees what happened looks on in horror and amazement. They can't believe that Hannibal and Li'l Timmy can actually be that bold.

But they are that bold. And so are the rest of the people that were in the meeting with Carlo.

Over a four day time period, this scenario repeats itself like a scene from Groundhog's Day in Harlem, Brooklyn, and the Bronx. The end result is over one hundred minor and mid-level players being taken out in both broad daylight and at night.

It doesn't take long for players in all boroughs of New York City to get shook. And, just as she desired, Tamika walks into a safe haven when she returns to New York.

CHAPTER TWO

Marley Regains His Old Notoriety

Marley and Tamika land at John F Kennedy Airport after a long and grueling flight. But it all seems worthwhile when Marley gets off the plane and notices how everyone treats him. They act like he's royalty.

"Hello, Sir," people say to him as they walk by.

Knowing that people rarely ever speak to strangers in New York City, Marley feels confident that his reputation is still intact. But he's totally unaware of the fact that a good portion of the goodwill that he's receiving is based on the fact that his daughter is with him and her crew has already softened up the streets before they arrived.

"Well, Dad, I guess you're still the man," Tamika says, stroking his ego. "Just look at the way that everybody's treating you."

"That's only because I haven't been here in a while," Marley says. "Believe me it'll wear off in time."

Tamika doesn't comment. She knows her dad well enough to pick up that even though he's being modest about it, he feels good about all the attention.

There's hope for him after all, Tamika thinks.

Marley heads straight for the Jamaican Embassy after dropping his things off at the Waldorf Astoria.

Tamika has other plans, though, and wants no parts of the old school festival. She pretends like she's going to rest, knowing that shortly after her dad leaves she'll be meeting with her squad.

****

Tamika is waiting in the lobby for Carlo to pick her up. Ordinarily she would take a Gypsy Cab but she wants to feel things out before making those types of moves.

Carlo pulls up in a Hummer and all Tamika can do is smile and shake her head. She runs outside and hops inside the Hummer, hugging Carlo once she's inside.

"Hey, Carlo, good to see you," Tamika says. "But didn't you learn anything from Frank Lucas about keeping a low profile?"

"You talking about the Hummer?" Carlo asks. "I'm not driving this for that reason. This is a real one like they use in wars. The metal is hard as shit and the windows are bulletproof. I just had it waxed up really good so that people wouldn't know the difference."

"If say so," Tamika says.

"For real, I'm not flossing," Carlo says. "I don't want to be the reason that makes everybody stop eating."

"It's cool. Forget about it," Tamika says. "Is everybody around?"

"Yeah. They're waiting for us at the spot in Brooklyn," Carlo says.

"Good." Tamika replies. "You know I want to look my entire squad in their eyes before I get too deep in bed with them."

"Well, they're all looking forward to seeing you," Carlo says.

"True that," Tamika replies.

For the remainder of the ride they each sit quietly, reflecting on things that are on their minds.

****

Tamika walks into the bar on 161st with Carlo and everybody stands up and applauds.

"Oh my God, Princess, it's good to see you," they say.

"It's good to see all of y'all," Tamika replies. "But sit down. I ain't that special. Y'all are the one's who need to be commended. I can tell that you've put in mad work out there in the streets. Niggas have been acting like it's the nineteen-sixties and they can't look us in the eyes when we approach them."

"We heard that's the way you wanted it, Ma," Hannibal says.

"You heard right and that's exactly how it is," Tamika says. "I'm proud of y'all. Y'all are making a bitch want to tear up and shit."

"Yeah, right, Tamika," Carlo says. "Like you're ever gonna cry."

"I can cry," Tamika says. "I cried when they killed Ramos." Tamika looks around to make sure that everyone in her squad believes her. "I cried when I had the miscarriage and lost his baby. I have emotions like everybody else."

"Well it's about to be all happy emotions," Hannibal says.

"You can believe that," says his partner Li'l Timmy.

"So Carlo, are you going to introduce me to everybody?" Tamika asks.

"Of course," Carlo says standing up. "The big guy and little guy are Hannibal and Li'l Timmy." He points them both out. "They get into so much shit together we tease them and call them a married couple. But don't get it fucked up. If you want havoc, you couldn't pick a better pair to make it happen."

Tamika speaks to Hannibal and Li'l Timmy and they speak back to her.

"This right here is John Carlo, our Italian assassin," Carlo says, continuing. "You know that every crew has to have its token Italian involved."

"Fuck you very much," John Carlo says.

"You're welcome," Carlo replies.

"This is Robert, Trusty, Stanley, Truth, Pete-Pete, Manney, Roger, Chris, Red Dot, and Amazon," Carlo says, pointing everybody out as he speaks.

Tamika exchanges pleasantries with everyone. Then she prepares to fill them in on as much specifics as she feels comfortable discussing about the operation. But first she wants to stroke their egos a little more.

"I wasn't kidding when I told y'all how impressed I am," Tamika says. "My dad felt so good while he was walking through the airport that he may even consider taking up a bigger roll again in the organization."

"Damn! Marley?" Carlo says. "That would be huge."

"That's what I saw in his eyes," Tamika says.
But even though she thinks that she is just saying what her crew wants to hear, Marley only attended a very quick meeting at the Jamaican Embassy regarding the festival before meeting with the heads of the Unity of Jamaican Brothers to reclaim his position at the head of the table.

"Well guys, I'm back," Marley says. "But I need to make sure that no one has a problem with me being in charge before I go any further."

No one says anything. They all want to eat off of Marley's plate.

"I'm sure y'all know that my daughter has softened up the entire city for us," Marley says. "She's such a fucking hothead. She doesn't know that I know but nothing gets by me. We need her level of ruthlessness at times. But don't anyone worry. I can control my daughter. She still answers

to me. And we will get a big piece of the Colombian cocaine pie. You can believe that."

Marley continues laying down the laws to the UOJB as
they listen intently. When he feels he's said enough for one
day, he wraps things up.

He goes to the door and hails his limousine driver.
Coming to America has made him feel special. And he's
soaking it up. He gets into the limousine as if he's royalty.

As old and wise as Marley is, he could learn a lot from
his daughter. A limousine ride is something that Tamika
would consider to be too risky. And he should also consider
it too risky.

Someone in his crew would have easily spotted the
green Ford Explorer with New Jersey license plates following the limousine from the Jamaican Embassy and noticed
that the same car is following them right now.

* * * *

Tamika gets back to the Waldorf Astoria and walks toward
the suite quietly. She thinks of a lie to tell her father about
where she's been but notices that she doesn't need to lie
once she opens the door. She's beaten him back.

The events of the day were so fulfilling, all Tamika
wants to do is relax and soak it all in.

She starts running a bubble bath and pops up a bottle of
Cristal to sip on while she's bathing.

Tamika dips her toe in the bat water after turning it off.

It's the perfect temperature. She leans her head back against the rubber pillow behind her head and reaches for the glass of Cristal that she's already poured.

"And nothing even matters at all," Tamika sings out loud along with Lauren Hill singing from the CD player.

Thump, thump, thump.

"Fuck! It never fails," Tamika says after hearing the knock at the door. "Every time I try to relax someone interrupts me. It's no wonder I'm not good at chilling out."

Tamika gets up and grabs a robe. She places it around her wet body and puts on her slippers.

"Coming," she says as she walks toward the door.

Tamika looks out of the peephole and sees the same harmless looking white man standing there that greeted Marley and her when they arrived earlier. Feeling assured, she opens the door.

"I have a package for Tamika Jefferson," says the concierge with a smile.

"Thanks. I wonder who this is from," Tamika says. "I'll bring you a tip when I come down."

"That's fine, Ma'am," the concierge says before tipping his hat and walking away.

Tamika looks at the package peculiarly as she places it on the table. Then she picks it up to shake it so she can ensure that she doesn't hear anything rattling around.

She doesn't.

Once her curiosity gets the best of her, she goes into her luggage and pulls out a pair of cuticle scissors. She uses them to cut away the packaging and rip into the box.

"Noooooooooooooooooooooooooooooooo," Tamika screams when she finally gets the box open.

She drops down to the floor crying and screaming hysterically.

Tamika keeps this up for over ten minutes until the hotel assistant manager starts knocking on her door.

"Ma'am is everything OK in there," he asks.

Tamika doesn't respond.

He looks at the female desk person and shakes his head.

"Use your key," he says. "We have to go in and find out what's going on."

They open the door and see Tamika kneeling on the floor rocking back and forth, still making way too much noise.

They walk towards her in an effort to console her. But before they reach her, the desk person can't help but look at the contents of the box.

"Oh my God1" the desk person hollers. "Do you see that?" she asks her supervisor.

He looks into the box and sees Marley's head, hands and tongue covered with blood.

Immediately, the assistant manager faints. The desk clerk doesn't panic. She picks up the room phone and tells her co-worker who answers to call the head of security and the police department up to the room she's calling from.
Next, she kneels besides Tamika and tries to comfort her.
But at this point only one thing will give her comfort — the

vengeance and revenge that's in her heart.

I'm going to kill any motherfucker that even looks like they had something to do with this, Tammy thinks.

People don't know it yet but everyone in New York City should be scared that Tammy has returned to take over Tamika's body. Pretty much anything is bound to happen now.

CHAPTER THREE

Tammy's Mission

"I can't believe this shit happened," Hannibal says to Carlo. "Now we have to bust some fucking heads to find out who's behind this."

"Yeah, all hell is pretty much about to break loose, and I don't plan on stopping y'all," Carlo says. "But just try to be calm when Tamika gets here. Feel her out. See what kind of frame of mind she's in."

"Yeah 'cause I heard that her temper is hotter than a motherfucker," Li'l Timmy says. "Right about now the slightest little thing will probably set her off."

Everyone quiets up when they see Tamika walk into the bar on 161st. She's wearing her Baby Phat shades to hide her red eyes.

Carlo stands up and gives her a caring hug.

"Hey Tamika," he says. "How'd you get here?"

"Call me Tammy," she replies quickly. "I have my

ways."

"I just want you to keep protocol," Carlo says, looking at Tamika weirdly. "We need to get more answers before we start taking any unnecessary chances."

"So who's up first?" Tamika asks, paying no mind to anything that Carlo has said. All she wants to know is what everyone has heard on the streets about her father's assassins.

"There're a couple crews that had to be dealt with after they didn't full cooperate with us," Carlo says. "You have the Latin Bombers, the Street Bangers, and the Bloods. But none of them would have any reason to come at your dad."

"And all of them are some - ass niggas," Tamika says. "They couldn't pull that shit off in a month of Sundays. But what about those Shower Posse motherfuckers? Isn't Quazi supposed to be in charge of them? I heard he's Rodman's cousin."

"Yeah, I think he is," Li'l Timmy says. "We can go snatch that nigga up right now."

"No. That's too easy," Tamika says. "I have a better way of handling things." She turns to Carlo. "Can you have a handful of rowdy niggas chill wherever the fuck Quazi hangs at? Everybody else should just try to lay low here. But don't let anybody get too drunk. We need sharp reflexes. Like it or not we're at war right now."

Tamika drives around for hours in the car with Hannibal and Li'l Timmy, telling them to turn right here or left there. But she never mentions what's really in her head.

Every five minutes, she calls Carlo to find out if anyone has heard anything about where Quazi's located.

"Still nothing, Ma," Carlo responds every time Tamika asks him.

"Well call me and let me know something," she says.

Eventually Tamika gets frustrated about the whole deal. She decides to take matters in a direction no one would expect.

"Drive to 117th and Malcolm X Boulevard," Tamika says.

"What's there?" Hannibal asks.

She shoots darts with venom at him from her eyes.

"We can find a good parking space and walk over to where we're going," Tamika says, ignoring Hannibal's question.

As instructed, Hannibal drives to 117th and Malcolm X Boulevard and finds a good place to park.

Tamika hops out the car, toting her pocketbook, and starts walking up Malcolm X Boulevard toward 118th. Hannibal and Li'l Timmy look at each other inquisitively before they follow her. In a couple seconds, they catch up.

"Nice of you to join me," Tamika says before changing the subject. "Look, when we go in here, let me do me. I'll handle everything. All I need y'all for is to wave your guns and flex a little muscle."

"Bet," Hannibal says.

Li'l Timmy doesn't comment. He just quietly follows Tamika up the stoop and into the building.

Tammy goes up one flight of stairs then stops in front of a door that has no number on it. It's been ripped off.

"Step to the side," she tells Hannibal and Li'l Timmy before tapping lightly on the door.

"Who is it?" a female voice from inside says.

"I'm delivering some medical supplies from Children's Harvest," Tamika says. "I hope this is the right place."

"Just one minute," the female voice from inside says. Once again Hannibal and Li'l Timmy look at each other clueless.

"I'm glad that y'all finally got here," the female says when she opens the door.

Quickly, reaches inside her pocketbook, pulls out a huge pair of metal pliers and whacks the woman across the face with them. She falls back into the house with a yelp.

"Shut it the fuck up!" Tamika demands after following the woman inside the house. "I swear the next loud sound you make will be your last. Now where's that motherfucker at?"

"Who? What are you talking about?" the woman asks.

Whack!

"Play me for a fucking fool, here?" Tamika snaps as the woman bites her tongue hard enough to draw blood so she doesn't make any noise.

"I swear I haven't seen Quazi," the woman says.

"You swear, huh?" Tamika asks. "We'll see about that."

Tamika walks toward the playpen that's sitting in the middle of the living room and lifts out the seven-year-old who would be too old to be in a playpen if he wasn't a retarded child.

She sits the boy on the floor directly across from the woman and gestures with the pliers for Hannibal and Li'l Timmy to come closer.

When they get close enough to the woman to hold her back if she moves, Tamika gets serious.

"So, like I said, you swear that you haven't seen him?" Tamika asks.

"Yes, I swear," the woman says. "He's always starting trouble so I asked him to stop coming around here."

"Is that right?" Tamika says sadistically.

While Hannibal and Li'l Timmy are looking like they're wondering what's about to happen next, Tamika bends down and grabs the little boy's lips with the pliers.

"I swear I'll twist his motherfucking lips so hard I'll make them go back fucking straight," Tamika snaps.

The little boy starts wailing in pain.

"Please don't hurt him," the woman says.

"Yeah, he ain't right," Hannibal says.

"Do you think I fucking give a damn about people thinking I don't have a heart after all the shit that I've been through in my life?" Tamika asks rhetorically. She isn't looking for an answer. "I swear I'll tear his motherfucking lips off if this bitch keeps playing with me."

The little boy continues to scream as blood begins to pour from his mouth.

"OK. OK," the woman says. "He's hanging out in a

eating spot down the street past 121st."

"How many guns?" Tamika hollers.

"There's usually four or five people sitting in SUV's outside," the woman says.

"Stay here and watch her," Tamika tells Li'l Timmy. "If she fucking sneezes, blast her ass. And if this little bastard doesn't stop crying in less than a minute, drawing attention to this apartment, you can blast his ass, too." She turns to Hannibal. "You and I are gonna ride there after we call for some more soldiers."

Hannibal follows Tamika out the door, finally realizing that she's indeed like the dominant female in a pack of African hyenas. She takes no prisoners and is all about her business.

* * * *

Everyone gets into position near the spot Quazi's hanging in above 121st. Tamika gives all the warriors in the vehicles around her the signal with her hands then she chirps the snipers that she has posted with rifles about a half block away.

"Now," she hollers into her Nextel.

Quickly three rifles fire six shots into the SUV's that Tamika and the crew are keeping tabs on. The inhabitants die at once.

Quickly, Tamika gets out the car and runs towards the restaurant. Everyone follows behind her.

Bang.

Tamika shoots Quazi in the leg as her entourage walks in behind her with guns drawn.

"Answers, motherfucker, answers!" Tamika screams at Quazi as he whines in pain.

"I don't know what you're talking about," he says.

Bang.

She shoots him again this time in his ankle.

"They're gonna kill me," Quazi says.

"If you think that I'm the one to play with you need to call your Grandmom and ask her about your retarded ass son," Tamika yells.

"What did you do to him?" Quazi asks.

"No. The question is what is my man about to do to him if you don't tell me what I want to hear in two seconds or less," Tamika screams.

Quazi doesn't answer fast enough so she chirps Li'l Timmy.

"Yo?" he answers.

"You know that retarded motherfucker that you're there with?" Tamika asks.

"Yeah, what's good?" Li'l Timmy asks.

"Wait, wait," Quazi says. "It was Escobar. He paid us for a hit. The Shower Posse ain't really have nothing to do with it. He says he was getting you back for doing in Ramos."

"For the last fucking time, I did not kill Ramos," Tamika screams to no one in particular. Then she calms her-

self down and looks at Quazi. "Thanks for the information."

Bang. Bang. Bang.

After shooting him three times in the head, she turns to
walk away but pauses when she gets to the door. She turns
back to Quazi.

"You faggot motherfucker," she says before walking
back to the car with Hannibal.

Hannibal has no idea what Tamika is about to do next.
He sits there twiddling his thumbs.

"I guess we're going to Colombia," Tamika says. "I
need to holla at Escobar about something."

CHAPTER FOUR

Posse Up

Carlo steers the car through the area of Brooklyn called DUMBO since it's situated down under the Manhattan Bridge overpass.

Tamika feels comfortable about meeting in DUMBO since it has so many huge warehouses and places to hide their cars.

"This would be a good area for you to move to, Tamika," Carlo says. "There's a lot of parks here. This is the perfect place to let a little boy run around acting crazy."

"Are we getting in people's business today?" Tamika asks.

"I'm just saying," Carlo replies.

"Well, first of all, no one said that I would have been having a boy in the first place," Tamika says. "But that doesn't matter since I'm not keeping it."

"How could you kill Ramos's baby?" Carlo asks.

"That's the only thing that we have left of him."

"No it's not," Tamika says. "We have so many good memories. Besides, he knew I was having an abortion," Tamika lies.

"You're lying, Tamika," Carlo says. "Ramos would have freaked if he found out you wanted to kill his baby."

"He didn't freak out because he thought I was going to change my mind," Tamika says. "But imagine me and my wild ass being pregnant. How the hell am I supposed to run around the way that I do with something in my belly?"

"That's why you need to just calm down," Carlo says. "How much money can you make anyway?"

"It's not always about money," Tamika says. "And right now all I'm worried about is avenging Marley's death. How the fuck can I even think about having a baby until that is done? Now, are you done minding my business today?"

Carlo doesn't comment. He knows that he isn't about to change Tamika's mind once she's made it up.

Truthfully speaking, if someone killed his father and he was as close to him as Tamika was to Marley, Carlo would be acting the same exact way.

Too bad that Carlo doesn't know his father. Most of the people in Tamika's crew don't know their fathers. The UOJB has provided all the guidance the troubled youngsters needed. Now it's Tamika's turn to act like their Momma.

* * * *

"Does everyone know why I picked this place?" Tamika asks all the men standing in front of her. No one answers her so she proceeds to tell them. "A little further down this block is Fulton Ferry. The first president of this country was evacuated from the Battle of Brooklyn on the Fulton Ferry. That means he was retreating. Our crew will never retreat. And we will never back down. I want everyone to know that as much as I want revenge for Marley, we have to make sure that the UOJB's name echoes through all the streets of New York. No one can think that we fell off just because my dad died. That means you all have to be visible in the streets. Everybody has to know their position."

Tamika scans the faces of all the men in front of her. Of course Carlo is her major. She views Hannibal and Li'l Timmy as the captains that help provide the muscle. They supervise Red Dot, Amazon, and Trusty who roam all the boroughs letting their faces be seen. John Carlo is the captain that maintains the good will with the Italian mob families in the city. And basically everyone else has been a good soldier to her despite not having an official position.

Tamika also has kinks in her crew's armor since her captain Sid Money is locked down at Riker's Island in the Vernon Bain Correctional Center and her lieutenant Jobbo is incarcerated at the Marcy Correctional Facility.

But Tamika knows in her heart that her crew won't be locked up for long. Jobbo is scheduled to be paroled in less than a month and although Sid Money still has several years left to serve, Tamika has no intention for him to completely pay the State of New York what the District Attorney believes he owes.

"Roger, I need for you to tighten up in Jamaica," Tamika says. "Maybe you can get Chris to handle Flushing or vice-versa. However you want to handle it but y'all can't be coming up short. If you need for Trusty to come lean on some people just let him know. He's a legend around there."

"Pete-Pete, I don't know what you're doing but I haven't heard a peep coming from Astoria, Queensbridge, or Jackson Heights," Tamika says, continuing. "Keep that shit up."

Tamika continues to guide her lieutenants on what to do in their boroughs. Robert is in charge of the Bronx. Stanley controls Brooklyn and Far Rockaway, Queens. Truth handles Long Island and Manney, Harlem. Basically, they hold a big stake in everything that happens in New York. And Tamika wants to make sure that they keep things that way.

"So, y'all just go out there and put your stamps on shit," Tamika says. "Red Dot, Amazon, and Trusty, y'all roam. I need to holla at Carlo, John Carlo, Hannibal, and Li'l Timmy."

All of the lieutenants disperse to patrol their neighborhoods while Tamika prepares to fill her major and captains in on her plan to bring Sid Money back into the fold.

"OK, so let's talk about Sid Money," Tamika says, once she's certain that only the top people in her crew remain.

"Are you back on that again?" Carlo asks. "He's on Riker's Island. It's basically a rap for him until it's time for his parole."

"You see, that's why as smart as you are, Carlo, I'm in charge and you're not," Tamika says. "There ain't shit that we can't do. We run this city and every person in it. Riker's may be what it is but it's run by the Department of Corrections. Ain't we making a fucking killing off our product in the prisons?" They all shake their heads. "Of course we are. That's because the Department of Corrections does what we say. And next week Sid Money is going to be transported off that damned barge and waiting for us at Queensboro Plaza. It'll be that simple. It ain't like he'll be under maximum security. All we have to do is get the Department of Correction to let up a little bit and before they know what happened, Sid Money will become someone else that's being scheduled for parole."

"You know what? That may actually work," John Carlo says. "Sometimes if you get the right CO's, you can get away with anything. Them boys be slippin."

"That's what I'm counting on," Tamika says.

"Well, I hope it works," Carlo says. "It sounds like you have it all planned out. I just don't want you to be put in jeopardy. How are you gonna pull this off. Sid Money has to play his roll in all of this."

"I know," Tamika says. "That's why I came down on the crew like I did today so I could make sure that everybody's shit is tight. And Hannibal and Li'l Timmy, I need y'all to go out there and reaffirm that shit. Carlo and I are gonna be gone most of the day and night."

"Gone where?" Carlo asks.

"I need for you to ride with me to Marcy," Tamika says.

"Jobbo can make sure the word gets to Sid Money faster than we can. And we won't be tied to Sid Money when everything goes down."

****

Tamika stretches her legs after taking the five-hour drive to Oneida County.

Carlo has pulled into an Amoco gas station and mini-market, which seems to be the perfect place for the two of them to spit up and go their separate ways.

Tamika is dressed very conservatively since she knows that many female visitors have been turned away from the Mid-State Correctional Facility in which the Marcy Correctional Facility is located. So, she opted to wear baggy jeans and a loose pullover sweatshirt.

The plan is for Carlo to head to the pool hall that is just a two-minute walk from the Amoco. Tamika, on the other hand, will wait around for a taxi. Under no circumstances does she want any of the straight-laced prison workers to get suspicious if they see Carlo and her together. In fact, with Carlo's rap sheet, just her being seen with him violates the conditions of her probation.

****

Tamika sits calmly waiting for Jobbo. Her legs are to-tally under the table and her hands are resting on the table. She's situated exactly how the guards have instructed her to be to insure that her visit isn't cut short.

When Jobbo arrives in his prison jumpsuit, Tamika doesn't get up. He assumes the exact sitting position as she is in but on the opposite side of the table.

"What's up, Jobbo?" Tamika says. "Long time no see."

"Too long," Jobbo replies.

"I hope you're not mad that I haven't visited before now," Tamika says.

"Nah, I know why," Jobbo says, calmly.

"Well, I'm fucking starving," Tamika says. "I bought this shit from the commissary but I was waiting for you to come so you can heat it up for me."

"I can tell that you ain't never been to Midstate," Jobbo says with a smile. "These guards ain't gon' let me do that. You have to go to the microwave yourself. They're worried that one of us would use that as a distraction to start some shit."

"Oh well, I guess I just have to get domesticated in prison," Tamika says as she walks over to the microwave with the prison guards keeping their eyes affixed on both Jobbo and her. After heating up her Oodles of Noodles and purchasing a can Pepsi for both Jobbo and herself, she strolls back over to the table and assumes the proper posi-tion. "I figured you wanted one too."

"Good looking," Jobbo says.

The meeting with Jobbo is brief. But it isn't so short that someone would get suspicious.

While speaking in code, Tamika informs Jobbo of her intentions to break Sid Money out of Riker's Island.

"Yeah, that dog was always getting spooked when the garbage truck pulled up in front of their house," Tamika says. "Even to this day I'm not sure if he can just relax and go with the flow when they come to pick up the trash."

"His ass better by now," Jobbo says. "I should try to find out the next time that I talk to his owners."

With that, Tamika knows that Jobbo has a C.O. at Marcy that also has to visit Riker's Island from time to time. The message will be delivered to Sid Money. All that's left to do now is continue the conversation with Jobbo until they pick a reasonable amount of time to cut the visit short.

****

Four days later Tamika is sitting inconspicuously in an eighty-seven Oldsmobile Cutlass Supreme inside the Queensboro Plaza 7 subway station parking area. She's wearing reading glasses and is skimming through the pages of the New York City Post.

Occasionally, she sips on the caramel latte that she purchased from Starbucks. But more than anything, she stays alert — glancing in her rearview and side mirrors with her peripheral vision so as not to deviate too much from the example being set by the other drivers that are reading about

New York City hot issues while scattered around in their cars waiting for passengers to exit the station.

Tamika feels confident that everything will work out because Hannibal and Li'l Timmy are on the Q101R bus that provides limited service to Rikers and Amazon is at the 21st St., Queensbridge F Subway Station. No one is certain where Sid Money will be dropped off but they are sure that they have every possible place accounted for so that they can steal Sid Money away as quickly as possible.

While Tamika and her crew are holding their positions, Sid Money is whispering to Greg Ingram. He's the prisoner who's supposed to be released.

"I told your ass not to panic," Sid Money says. "Just be calm and you'll be out of here in a couple days."

"But are you sure I won't get in trouble?" Greg asks. "They could charge me with conspiracy to defraud the system or something like that."

"Nigga, you don't even know how to spell defraud let alone know what it means," Sid Money says. "All you have to say is that you were in fear of your life. I threatened you at the last minute and forced you to help me. The guards know how much pull I have here. Everybody will believe that you were just scared shitless."

"I hope you're right," Greg says.

"I know I'm right," Sid Money replies. "'Cuz if I'm wrong and something doesn't work out you know that you'll never leave this prison alive."

Greg is positive that Sid Money means what he says so

he has no intentions on double-crossing him.

"Prisoner 9-3-0-0-6-4-5!" shouts a C.O.

The real Greg Ingram sits quietly as his number is called. Sid Money answers the C.O. and steps forward.

Shackles are placed on his wrist and a chain is placed on his legs as Sid Money is escorted off the barge and unto a powerboat.

Minutes later, Sid Money finds himself in out-processing and doesn't believe how smoothly everything is going.

"Ingram… Ingram!" shouts a C.O.

"Yeah," Sid Money says finally after snapping out of his daze. He almost forgot that his name is Greg Ingram.

"Hey, you can stay here all fucking day for all I care," says the C.O.

"My bad," Sid Money replies. "I was just thinking about being with my girl, that's all."

"Well, your girl is definitely somebody else's girl by now as long as you've been in here," the C.O. says, laughing. "So your ass needs to just pay attention so you can get on this fucking shuttle. Unless you want to wait four more hours before the next one comes."

"Nah, this one would be fine," Sid Money says. Sid Money is escorted onto a shuttle that drives to the South End of Riker's Island. When the driver reaches his destination, he brings the shuttle bus to a halt.

"This is as far as I go," the driver says.

Sid Money and several other passengers exit through the gates of Riker's Island and walk towards Queensboro

Plaza 7.

Once inside the parking lot, Sid Money scans all of the cars to see either a car or person driving that looks familiar. When he gets to the eighty-seven Cutlass Supreme, not even the disguise she's wearing can stop Sid Money from recognizing Tamika's pretty face.

Sid Money eases his way over to the vehicle and snatches the passenger side door open quickly.

"Hah, you were scared shitless," Sid Money says, laughing.

"No, I think that your ass was about to be a statistic," Tamika says as she raises the New York City Post enough to show Sid Money the Colt 45 revolver that she was hiding.

"And I was just standing over there thinking that you are one beautiful lady," Sid Money says. "How can someone so pretty be so vicious?"

"Those are the rules of the jungle, man," Tamika says. "Now get in here and give me a hug so we can get ghost. We ain't got no time for fun and games. We need to get back to fucking Harlem where it's safe."

CHAPTER FIVE

The Lock Down

"Now we need to raise some hell out here on these streets before I head to Colombia," Tamika says. "Since Amazon and Trusty are coming with me, Sid Money and Jobbo will be taking their places. I don't think that any of you feels like it will be a step down on muscle with those wild-ass niggas. Jobbo will be home shortly and he's ready to step right in." Tamika turns to Hannibal and Li'l Timmy. "I need for y'all to back off of the real gutter shit and let Sid Money handle it. Not only do the streets need to be reminded about him. But I need for y'all to be insulated from any snitches on the streets. They're already looking for Sid Money anyway so at this point some more shit added to his jacket at gon' hurt."

"Yeah, 'cuz I ain't stepping one foot back in nobody else's prison," Sid Money says. "Whatever Jake comes at me better know that his ass is going to hell right along with mine."

"I hear that," Li'l Timmy says jovially. "There ain't no other way to do it for gangsters like us."

* * * *

Truth and Red Dot sit inside a car parked in the Sagamore Hill section of Long Island. They watch as Sid Money struts over towards Dough Boy, a major player in Long Island that's refused to share the ball courts with Tamika's crew no matter how many times that she had them try to pressure him.

Sid Money has only one thing in mind as he confronts Dough Boy, that is, his time is up.

"Dough Boy, I've heard many things about you," Sid Money says.

"Same here," Dough Boy says. "I hear you're a legend in these parts."

Although Dough Boy is scared shitless, he feels confident that nothing can go down right now since there are so many people on the streets of Sagamore Hill.

"Truth was telling me that you don't like us," Sid Money says. "He says that you think that you're better than us."

"Nah man, it ain't that," Dough Boy says. "I'm just used to doing my own thing. It ain't nothing personal."

"We all like doing our own thing," Sid Money says. "But how could we sustain the race if we didn't combine with other people? You and I wouldn't be here if our parents didn't get together. You just don't jump on board with anybody but you have to get on board with somebody or the world leaves you behind."

"The world's been doing me just fine," Dough Boy says.   "Being by myself has its privileges."

"I know one privilege it doesn't have," Sid Money says.

"What privilege is that?" Dough Boy asks.

Sid Money whips out his heat.

Bang. Bang. Bang.

He shoots Dough Boy dead in front of everybody on the streets of Sagamore Hill.

"Eternity," Sid Money shouts loudly. "Being with us gives you the privilege of eternity."

The innocent bystanders on the streets scream, holler, run, and some duck behind cars for protection. But Sid Money isn't worried about any of them. He's already accomplished his directive for Long Island.

Sid Money casually strolls over to the car where Truth and Red Dot are waiting for him.

"You could've covered your face or something," Red Dot says.

"Nah, what would be the point?" Sid Money asks. "Everybody already knows who I am. I'm a dead man walking — an escaped convict that's ruthless as a motherfucker. You think any of those people are gonna remember anything? Please. The cops will have better luck getting them to remember their A, B, C's. I'm good. Let's get over to Jamaica. Roger is waiting for us."

Red Dot drives the car towards Jamaica, Queens after dropping Truth off. All is quiet in the car with regards to conversation. But the radio is pumping out hip-hop music like the fellas are on their way to a concert.

There will be no concerts today, though. What they have on their minds is more like a training session. Sid Money does not own a kennel but he has every intention to break the will of any of his dogs on the street that don't fall into line. And they'd all better beware because Tamika knew exactly what she was doing when she had Sid Money broken out of Riker's Island. She unleashed the beast of New York who knows how to dish out his own style of justice.

****

It's about two p.m. by the time Red Dot and Sid Money reach Jamaica, Queens and assemble the troops. Sid Money knows that he doesn't have much time since the police presence on the streets normally increases for a couple hours after school lets out.

Sid Money addresses everyone but his main targets are Tonkman Joey, the soldier that's always gambling, and Rasta Rick, a Montego Bay, Jamaican born illegal alien.

"Tamika is not happy about y'all always coming up short," Sid Money says. "I've never met somebody that stuck up for her crew as much as she does. She makes sure that everybody eats. And I know she's always throwing bonuses around like it ain't shit. So, I can't figure out for the life of me why y'all want to do her like that."

"We love the rude gal," Rasta Rick says. "But she's too removed from the everyday operations on the streets. We have cops coming at us for brides all the time. And sometimes we have to throw our stashes down the sewage drains before the Jakes hem us up. But Roger doesn't care. He wants everything. He never wants to hear our reasons why for what happened to make us short. I just figured that the rude gal leans on him so he leans on us."

"Bro, I know the numbers game with Tamika," Sid Money says. "All that shit you just talked about is factored into her equation for what kickback she expects from y'all. I don't even need to know what her expectations are now but I'm sure it's fair. That's just the type of person that she is."

"You don't understand, Man," Rasta Rick says.

"Bro, can I finish talking about what needs to happen around here or what?" Sid Money asks.

"I was just saying…"

Bang. Bang.

"You was just saying that you's a disrespectful mother-fucker," Sid Money snaps after shooting Rasta Rick twice in his right hand. "If your ass can't count right with your right hand then maybe you should be using your left hand. Or let me find out that your ass is just tired of counting the right way, period."

"No, Man, I can count right," Rasta Rick says while holding his right hand with his left one.

"You'd better," Sid Money hisses. "Because I'm not in the mood to be having this conversation again." He turns to the rest of the soldiers. "Does anyone else have anything to say?" There's complete silence. "Well, y'all better get back to your real estate and start collecting that cheddar. I already know that the count will be right."

While Red Dot and Sid Money finish up their conversation with Roger, Tonkman Joey lingers around next to their car. In a few minutes they walk over towards him.

"I was wondering if y'all can drop me off in Jackson Heights," Tonkman Joey says.

"Nigga, what the fuck is you, special?" Red Dot asks jokingly.

"Nah, Man, that's a long hike, that's all," Tonkman Joey says. "And I needed to holla at Sid Money about something anyway," he whispers.

"Alright then get your diva ass in the car then, Nigga," Sid Money says.

The remaining soldiers and Roger laugh at the joke. They have no idea about Tonkman Joey's desire to have a private conversation with Sid Money.

"So, what's on your mind?" Sid Money asks after they pull off.

"I know everybody thinks that I be fucking up," Tonkman Joey says.

"That's because you do be fucking up," Red Dot says, interrupting.

"Alright, I do fuck up," Tonkman Joey says. "But I

don't fuck up as much as y'all think I do."

"Let the man talk, Red Dot," Sid Money says. "We may need to hear what he has to say."

"Ok, then, talk Tonkman," Red Dot says.

"Well, sometimes when I play Tonk I may lose a little something," Tonkman Joey says. "But I never bet the money I have to turn in. I swear on everything that I love. So I may go to Roger and ask for a loan. If he wants to pull tech, he can when it's time for him to collect. But if I'm supposed to give him three-hundred-dollars for a package that's exactly what I give him."

"Then why are you short, then," Sid Money asks.

"Because I may owe him a hundred dollars," Tonkman Joey says. "So, I'll give him three-hundred-fifty-dollars and tell him I'll give him his other fifty bucks a little later. Then, instead of him giving Tamika the whole three-hundred, he'll give her two-fifty and tell her that I was short fifty."

"That fifty dollars that you owe him ain't got shit to do with the package money," Sid Money says.

"That's exactly my point," Tonkman Joey replies. "Roger be on some bullshit. And I'm not the only one that he does it to. We be loving it when he has something to do and Chris comes over here. On those days we don't have no problems."

Red Dot pulls over on 82nd St. in Jackson Heights to let Tonkman Joey out the car.

"Listen, I'm gonna look into that shit," Sid Money says.

"But you keep this conversation to yourself in the meantime."

"No doubt," Tonkman Joey says.

He gives Red Dot and Sid Money a pound and goes about his business.

The two men drive around Jamaica, Queens for a couple hours speaking with the soldiers. Sure enough, things are described to them in the same way that Tonkman Joey spoke of. After hearing enough, Sid Money gets Red Dot to take him back to Harlem so he can meet up with Tamika.

"So how are the streets?" Tamika asks after opening up the door and letting Sid Money in.

"I'm sure that the streets are humming by now," Sid Money says proudly. "A nigga's been putting in some work."

"I heard," Tamika says. "It's so sad to hear about Dough Boy."

"I know," Sid Money says. "He was so young. It's tragic. They need to do something about the violence on these streets."

Tamika and Sid Money start laughing for a few moments until they finally compose themselves.

"For real, though, Ma, I need to talk to you about sumthin'," Sid Money says.

"What?" Tamika asks. "I thought everything went the way we expected."

"It did," Sid Money says. "But you know how the streets be talking. You find out some good shit."

"Aw, damn. What's going on now?" Tamika asks.

"Let's just say that Jamaica isn't coming up short all the time because of the soldiers," Sid Money says. Tamika lifts her eyebrows up as if she can't wait for him to finish dishing the dirt. "The problem seems to be with the leadership. Some people don't seem to know the difference between a soldier owing them money and owing money on a package."

"You must be talking about Roger," Tamika says. "I could've sworn I already discussed this with him."

"Well it went in one ear and right out the other," Sid Money says. "I spoke to a bunch of soldiers separately and they were all singing the same tune. Roger is dancing to the beat of his own drummer. I think I may need to holla at his ass."

"No, you know good and well that unless a lieutenant puts you on the spot in front of a bunch of the soldiers I have to deal with him personally," Tamika says.

"I know," Sid Money says. "But a nigga like that makes me mad as hell. He has the world at his feet and still has to act greedy. You know the nigga only gave his soldiers a thousand off that million-dollar bonus you gave him."

"You know what…" Tamika says before pausing. "I never did feel the love in Jamaica or Flushing that I feel from the rest of my squad. Take my phone and chirp Chris and Roger while I change my clothes. I need to meet up with everybody."

Tamika goes into her room and grabs one-hundred-thousand-dollars out of her safe. Then she puts on a pair of tight Baby Phat jeans to further amplify her sexiness.

She grabs her matching Baby Phat purse and sticks a thirty-eight special into it before walking out of her room and joining Sid Money.

"Is everything set up?" she asks.

"Yeah, they're waiting on us," Sid Money says.

****

Carefully, Tamika drives back to Jamaica, Queens with Sid Money riding shotgun.

She stops the car in front of a bar on Forest Hills. The Flushing and Jamaica, Queens crews meet there all the time because it's almost midway between the two territories.

Tamika gets out the car and starts walking with a sexy swagger. She knows that she has to win her crews heart back any way that she can before leaving for Colombia.

"I just wanted to meet with all of y'all to have a drink because honestly I haven't been feeling the love," Tamika says to all the soldiers while Chris, Roger, and Sid Money look on. She turns to the bartender. "Let me get a shot of Hennessey for everybody."

The rumbling in the group lets Tamika know that at least they are on the path to becoming happy. But she knows that she'll have to do a little more to seal the deal.

"To the UOJB," Tamika says while holding her shot of Hennessey up in the air.

"To the UOJB," everyone repeats her and mimics her actions by holding their shots in the air as well.

They down their shots in unison then try to place manly expressions on their faces.

"Another round, Bartender," Tamika says before turning back to the soldiers. "Seriously, though. There's another reason that I wanted all of you to meet me here. I have something for you all. You've been doing a good job on the streets and I recognize that. I know I get mad when the count is short and y'all are gonna work on that, but I also know that I have a good crew. That's why I have a gift for everybody."

One by one Tamika has the soldiers come up to her so she can hand them five-thousand-dollars apiece. When she gets to Chris, she hands him twenty-five-thousand.

Roger, though, doesn't receive cash. For him, Tamika only has a lecture.

"You know, Roger, I wouldn't have to be reeling your people back in if you were doing a better job of controlling things," Tamika says.

"But…" Roger says before being cut off.

"No buts," Tamika says. "Just let your people enjoy their moment so shit can get tightened up in Jamaica and Flushing. With all that money out there, we should be making a killing. I don't want your count to come up short again at all. I can't even believe that we're still having these conversations."

Tamika gestures to Sid Money then gets up off of her barstool. They walk out the door leaving the Flushing and Jamaica soldiers to their celebration.